THE PRINCE AND THE SERPENT

Volume 1

AMULET KARLOW

ISBN: 979-8-89079-449-9 (hardcover)
ISBN: 979-8-89079-450-5 (paperback)
ISBN: 979-8-89079-451-2 (ebook)

CHAPTER 1
THE DAWN

Steel rang in the training court—a bright, slicing note that sent sparrows skittering from the garden wall. The morning air still carried the cool damp of dawn, smelling faintly of oil and iron from freshly scrubbed stones. James dipped under the arc of a wooden practice blade, wind curling around his ankles like a living thing. He let it lift him half a breath, slid past his opponent's guard, and landed a precise tap at the hollow of a throat.

"Again," he said, breath easy, eyes laughing.

Master Orin's jaw tightened. He was sweating. James wasn't. Around the perimeter, squires leaned their elbows on the railing, whispering wagers they should not have placed within earshot of the royal apartments.

"Prince James!" someone hissed. "Your father is watching."

Up on the balcony, the Hero King stood with hands clasped behind his back, posture straight as a pike. Sunlight netted his golden hair and set it blazing; the same color burned in James's—a mirror he had never asked for. The King spoke quietly to an attendant, already pointing, already instructing. He didn't wave. He didn't need to. Everyone bent toward him anyway.

James's smile became strained.

Orin feinted high. Wind gathered where James's heel kissed earth—barely a ripple—and the feint died against an invisible current. James turned the strike aside, stepped in, and finished the bout with a clean shoulder-check that sent the veteran master stumbling.

Gasps. A smattering of cheers. Even a few laughs.

Sarah did not laugh.

She materialized at the stairwell in ash-red robes, braid swinging like a warning. "You promised to stop bullying the training staff," she said—voice even, eyes very much not.

"I promised to stop bullying the *young* training staff." James offered Master Orin a hand up. "He's ancient."

"I'm thirty-five," Orin muttered.

"Exactly," James said, and Sarah's elbow found his ribs with suspicious accuracy.

Her gaze snagged on the air around his wrists, where magic still glimmered faintly—wild and eager.

"You're leaking," she said. "Again."

"It's windy," he replied, throwing her a grin.

"The wind doesn't follow you like a dog," she shot back. "Also, Lady Anne wants you both for reading after lunch. Don't be late."

"Reading?" Ben groaned from the nearest bench without getting up. He was halfway horizontal already, long legs draped over the armrest, brown hair in his eyes. "Truly? We just watched James dismantle a legend. I say we eat, nap, and reflect."

"You say 'nap' and 'reflect' like they're different activities," Sarah said dryly.

Ben considered, then shrugged. Sarah rolled her eyes.

James flipped his practice blade to a squire and scooped his cloak from the railing in one easy motion. Beyond the court, Valenor basked: pennants breathing on the palace towers, medicinal gardens exhaling sweet pungency, healed soldiers trading patched-together stories under the colonnade. The city had learned to mend. The kingdom wore its scars like filigree.

"Your Highness," Orin said, formal again, "there's very little left I can do for you."

"I know," James said lightly.

But the words settled in his stomach with a familiar clink. Another master done. Another lesson ending where it always did—with people glancing to the balcony, with praise that somehow bent toward someone else.

The morning slid forward. In the library, Sarah read dry treatises aloud and tested him without warning. He answered them all because answers came easily; everything did. Ben fell asleep in a chair with a book open over his face like a dignified tombstone. When the bells tolled the second hour after noon, James shut the tome on ancient forbidden magics and watched dust lift in the light.

"Done?" Sarah asked. "This topic is the most important. Stories always say the most dangerous magic isn't forbidden because it's powerful," she muttered, flipping her own text closed. "It's forbidden because someone had to stop it."

"Sealed by earth, guarded by fire," Ben recited absently from beneath his book. "My grandmother used to say that whenever she hid the cookie jar."

"Yeah, yeah," James muttered with a wave of his hand. He had heard it all before. "Anyway, I am done with the book." He tipped his chair back, balancing. "But with the day? Not nearly."

Her eyes narrowed. "No."

"You don't even know what I'm going to say."

"You're going to say you're bored." She stood, eyes stern and promising future wrath. "And then you're going to say you had an idea."

He flashed teeth. "I had an idea."

"Ben," she called without looking away from James, "if you care for your continued survival, talk him out of it."

From beneath his book, Ben's voice drifted: "Talking is strenuous."

James pushed to his feet. "It's just… one little improvement to the statue."

"The last improvement involved paint," Sarah said. "And pigeons. And an ambassador with a feather phobia."

"The pigeons were an accident." He tugged on his cloak. The itch under his skin—restless, directionless—demanded a target. The Hero King commanded everything: councils, patrol schedules, even the angle of the palace hedges. James could best every test and still hear it—the quiet comparison, the unspoken checklist that tallied him up as his father's shadow.

He needed air.

They left the library with James in the lead and Sarah and Ben reluctantly following.

They cut through market streets strung with drying herbs. Vendors called out blessings to the prince—good health, bright winds, soft landings. He tossed coins where he could, tipped his chin where he couldn't, aware of how sunlight hit his hair and made strangers sigh like a prophecy had just walked past. Somewhere, a pair of children argued whether his eyes were really the color of the sky or just very clean water.

He should have found it charming.

"Don't," Sarah warned, catching his sleeve as he reached for a discarded rope near a tailor's awning.

"I was only thinking," he said.

"I know. That's why I stopped you."

"You are no fun," he said, dropping the rope.

"I am the reason you still have kneecaps," she answered.

The statue rose in the square—bronze, gleaming, eternal.

The Hero King lifted his sword toward a peaceful sky. Pigeons sat on his shoulders like medals. Once, their shared hair and eyes had been an omen of disaster. Now people rubbed the statue's foot for luck and tucked flowers into its palms.

Hope had a face.

Not his.

James swallowed around something thorny and kept walking.

"Ben," he said suddenly, "wake up."

Ben appeared at his elbow, entirely awake. "I never slept."

"Good. Because I've thought of something better than paint."

Sarah groaned. "Your birthday feast is next week. Diplomats will be here. Dignitaries. People who can declare war if offended."

"Then we'll be selective about who sees it," James said smugly.

"Or we could not do it at all," Sarah offered.

"That seems excessive."

They argued all the way back. He sent Sarah off with a promise he had no intention of keeping ("I'll behave," which made her snort) and dragged Ben to the top of the east tower, where the wind licked at their clothes and the whole of the capital city of Solis lay open like a map.

"Okay," Ben sighed. "Let's hear it."

James spread his hands. "Illusion. A perfect one. Timed with the fireworks. Something the court mages can't dismiss."

Ben stared. "You're smiling. That's never a good sign."

"Minimal risk," James promised. "Maximum effect."

"Sarah will murder us," Ben said.

"She'll try."

The wind rose to meet him, warm and familiar. For the first time all day, the pressure eased.

When everything was effortless, it was impossible to tell what was worth holding onto.

———————————————————————————————

The day before his eighteenth birthday dawned bright and expectant. James rose with it, giddy with excitement. His plan was devised; all was ready—he just needed a couple of supplies.

He dressed quickly in pink and gold and slipped through the quiet halls, careful not to be seen. Showing initiative before dawn would cause panic among the staff.

He reached Ben's room unhindered.

Ben slept sprawled across half the bed, blankets a hopeless tangle. James smirked. He could tap-dance across the floor and Ben wouldn't twitch.

He took a breath.

"Wake up!" he bellowed, leaping onto the mattress with both feet.

Ben launched skyward with a strangled noise, limbs flailing, eyes enormous.

"James—what—*why*—?!"

"I told you dawn," James said, hands on hips.

"This is such a—" Ben flopped back onto the bed "—drag."

"We have to go, or Nanny-Sarah will catch us."

"Assuming you didn't wake her already," Ben muttered.

James kicked his shoulder lightly. "Up."

Ben shoved his hair out of his eyes and glared. "Get out so I can get dressed."

"I'm not looking," James said, already turning away. "If I stand outside, I'll get caught. Besides, I'm not interested in *you*."

A pillow hit the back of his head.

"I know that. Aren't you supposed to marry Sarah?" Ben's voice carried just enough teasing to be dangerous.

"Don't remind me," James groaned. "Everyone knows I don't like her like that. She doesn't like me like that either."

Ben went quiet, sympathy softening the air.

"Maybe they think—"

"They're wrong," James said sharply. Then, softer: "It's my choice."

He pushed the mood away and hopped back onto the bed.

"You ready yet?"

Another sigh. "Yes."

"Excellent," James declared, spinning to face him. "Adventure awaits."

The pillow hit his face this time.

"Get off my bed!"

CHAPTER 2
THE ARCANE MAGE

On the east side of Solis, where cobblestone lanes dissolved into wild grass and the air grew damp beneath the forest's shadow, stood a lonely thatched-roof hut. Its roof sagged under years of storm-worn seasons, and its smudged windows hid behind curtains that never once stirred. Smoke drifted in a thin, unbroken ribbon from the narrow chimney, staining the mossy stone black and perfuming the clearing with cedar and the metallic tang of enchantments left too long unattended.

Here lived Sahir the Hermit.

Or rather—*existed.*

No one remembered when he had come to Solis. Some whispered he had been there before the first city walls, watching silently as foundations were laid. Others swore he had appeared one winter during the war, walking out of the forest with nothing but a staff and a jar of captured light. Whatever the truth, he had remained—unchanged—year after year. His name carried through taverns, barracks, and market stalls like a rumor that refused to fade: *the mage who could make any wish possible... for a price.*

It was precisely that reputation that drew Prince James to his door.

He moved quickly down the narrow path, cloak brushing wet grass and boots sinking into soft mud. The woods hushed around him, swallowing his footsteps. Somewhere behind him, a sparrow trilled once, then fell silent—as though even the birds knew sound did not belong here.

The hut loomed ahead, unchanged from the last time he'd seen it.

He had only come once before, years ago, when he, Ben, and Sarah had dared each other to touch its moss-dark stones. He remembered it in fragments: pine needles underfoot, the cold shadow beneath the eaves, the prickling certainty that something unseen had turned to look at him. That same sensation crawled now along his skin like static.

He forced his shoulders straight, plastering on a grin he did not feel.

"Come on, Ben," he called, glancing back at the friend who trailed several paces behind. "Don't tell me you're scared."

Ben straightened immediately, affronted. "I'm not scared. I'm cautious. There's a difference."

James smirked. "Sure. Whatever you say."

"This is such a drag," Ben muttered, quickening his pace.

James raised his fist to knock—then paused. The air thickened around him, heavy and expectant, as though the hut itself held its breath. He reminded himself he had plenty of gold, more than enough to pay for whatever Sahir demanded. He was brave enough. He had made up his mind.

He knocked.

One minute passed.

Then two.

Then three.

"Maybe he's not home."

The unexpected voice jolted through him like a bolt. He whipped around so fast his neck cracked. Ben's face was inches from his own—close enough their cheeks nearly collided.

"Damn it, Ben! Don't scare me like that!" James clutched his chest, heart thundering. Ben only raised a brow, unimpressed, likely savoring revenge for the dawn wake-up.

James opened his mouth to berate him—but froze.

Ben wasn't looking at him anymore.

His gaze was fixed on the door.

It was cracked open.

"Hey, it opened," James murmured.

Instinct tugged hard—*stop, leave, turn back*—but curiosity and stubbornness trampled it. He stepped forward.

Ben seized his shirt, yanking him back. "James, you shouldn't—"

But James was already reaching forward.

"Let's check it out."

The hinges groaned as he pushed the door wider. A rush of air slid past them—dry, herbal, faintly metallic. Shadows flickered along the walls from a hearth in the left wall where a small iron pot simmered. It smelled of stew layered over something sharper, acrid, alive.

Ben lingered at the doorway, unease radiating from him.

James walked inside.

"Hello?" he called. "Is anyone here?"

Only the pop of a collapsing log answered.

He stepped deeper, boots whispering over rough boards. Shelves lined the room from floor to ceiling, crammed with jars—hundreds of them—each labeled in cramped, precise script that glimmered faintly in the firelight. Bundles of herbs dangled from the rafters, and delicate glass tools lay scattered across cluttered tables. Strange as it was, the space felt lived-in, not abandoned.

Ben's whisper was sharp. "James, we should go. Now."

"Maybe I can just find what I need," James murmured.

Ben stared at him. "You can't rob a mage!"

"I'm not robbing anyone," James said, offended. "I'll leave the gold where he'll see it. Triple the price if it makes you feel better."

He scanned the shelves, muttering as he searched: powdered basilisk scales, wind crystal…

Then the air changed.

A violent wind tore through the room, rattling jars and whipping herbs into a frenzy. Dust burned his eyes; the fire flared green. James shielded his face and shouted, "Ben!"—but the roar swallowed his voice.

Through the chaos, he saw Ben hurled backward by invisible force—launched through the open door into daylight. The door slammed shut behind him with a thunderous crack.

Silence dropped like a hammer.

James lunged for the door, yanking with all his strength. It didn't move.

"Ben!" he yelled, pounding his fists against the wood.

From the other side came muffled shouting and the dull thud of Ben trying to break in.

Then—another voice.

Smooth as silk.

Cold as winter water.

"What," it asked, "are you doing here?"

James spun.

A tall figure stood by the fire, half-turned toward him. A dark brown robe draped to the floor, long black nails with square tips tapping idly against the velvet armchair. His hood hung low, hiding his features—until the firelight caught the edge of a pale jaw.

James's breath hitched.

"Sahir," he whispered.

The mage lifted one slender hand and pulled back his hood with a fingernail. Sleek black hair spilled down his back like pouring ink.

James stared. Sahir waited.

"I—I'm—"

"The Prince?" Sahir finished. "I know."

His voice was calm, almost gentle. "What I want to know is what business Prince James has in my home."

James swallowed. The room felt smaller.

"I need ingredients."

Sahir nodded once, as if he already knew. He waited.

"Powdered basilisk scales… and a wind crystal."

Silence answered him—thin, stretching, dangerous.

Sahir finally turned. The firelight revealed eyes of pure black—endless, depthless, hungry. His expression shifted from curiosity to something sharper.

"Rare items," he murmured, gliding to a shelf. "And dangerous."

"I have gold—"

"I have something else in mind."

He lifted a small jar, stroking it with unsettling fondness.

"In exchange for what you seek, allow me to give you a gift."

James froze.

Sahir was drifting closer—much too close.

Instinct screamed and finally he obeyed.

James pivoted, slamming his shoulder into the door. It held. Ben's muffled shouts continued outside, frantic and distant.

James reached for his knife.

Sahir was faster.

A black-tipped hand clamped around his wrist. Acid-green magic circles ignited across the walls, the floor, the ceiling—overlapping, spinning, pulsing. James twisted violently, fighting with everything he had, but Sahir held him effortlessly.

The green light intensified.

Sahir crushed the jar in his palm. Glass splintered. Blood trailed over his fingers. He did not flinch.

"With this mark, your fate is clear," he chanted, voice warping, echoing, swelling.

James's stomach plummeted.

A curse.

Sahir forced open his hand.

"Pay heed. Eyes the color of the sky now belong to another..."

He shoved the jar's bloody contents into James's palm. The glass shards sliced his flesh.

Pain ripped through him—molten, electric, searing up his arm like fire poured straight into his veins. James screamed, though even he couldn't hear it over the roaring wind.

"And your talent will be your undoing."

The world exploded in white.

His body convulsed. The curse carved itself deep—

And then—

Silence.

When he woke, he was lying face-down in the dirt.

Warm sunlight baked his back. The smell of earth, grass, and ashes tickled his nose. The air was quiet—peaceful in a way that felt wrong.

He pushed himself upright, limbs trembling.

The hut was gone.

Only scorched earth and some stones remained, still smoking.

"Ben?" he croaked. "Ben!"

He stumbled forward until he found him—unconscious in the rubble, tossed aside like debris from a storm. James dropped to his knees and shook him.

A groan. Eyelids fluttering.

Relief washed through him so sharply it hurt.

Ben's focus sharpened—and then widened in horror.

"James… What the hell happened to you?!"

"I… don't know," James whispered.

His voice sounded distant. His mind felt hollow, echoing.

His sleeve had burned away to the elbow. His skin was darkened, soot-streaked, trembling.

But the true damage lay in his hand.

A perfect black rune was etched into his palm.

Its edges shimmered faintly—alive, pulsing with lingering magic.

James stared until his vision blurred.

Pain didn't come.

Just a terrible, absolute certainty:

Nothing would ever be the same.

CHAPTER 3
CURSED

By the time they reached the city gates, James and Ben must have looked every bit as awful as they felt.

Mud clung to their boots, soot streaked their faces, and both boys leaned into each other like drunks staggering home after a particularly nasty bar fight. The difference was that drunks rarely carried a curse on their hands—or the fear that the King of Valenor might be waiting at the other end.

Ben grunted under James's weight as they limped through the cobbled streets. "Can you at least try to walk? You're heavier than you look," he muttered.

"I *am* walking," James protested, though his legs told a different story. His left arm was slung across Ben's shoulders, his injured hand clutched close to his chest. Every heartbeat sent a pulse of heat through the mark on his palm, like a brand refusing to cool.

They must have made quite the spectacle. Women gasped behind gloved hands; men shouted for guards; a baker nearly dropped his tray of bread. Whispers followed them through the square—half concern, half scandal. The prince was bleeding in broad daylight.

"Great..." James muttered to himself as the guards rushed over. He was really going to hear it from his dad.

Ben shot him a look that could have curdled milk. "*Your dad?!*" Ben cried, sounding incredulous. James belatedly realized he had said that out loud. "You, the Crown Prince, were injured on *my* watch. My mom is going to kill me!"

James winced—not from pain, but guilt. Lady Simone's temper was legendary; her disappointment even worse. Ben wasn't joking. "Sorry. I'll talk to her," he offered.

Ben groaned. "No! That'll only make it worse. *Damn. It!*" Ben lamented his fate and existence respectively.

Before James could reply, the city guards appeared—six of them in polished armor, eyes widening as they recognized the prince. One barked orders; another ran ahead toward the palace, shouting for Lady Anne. The rest surrounded them in a protective formation, ushering the boys forward. James tried to wave them off, but the effort only made the mark on his palm throb harder.

"Ge'off, I can walk. It's not bad," James protested weakly as he tried to push them away. He was ignored as they pulled him off of Ben.

One guard—an older man with a scar down his jaw—gave him a weary look. "With respect, Your Highness, it looks plenty bad."

And that was the end of that.

The grand doors of the palace opened before them like the mouth of a waiting beast. James had always loved this place—its marble corridors and sunlit arches—but today the familiar halls felt colder. Servants froze mid-step as the group passed, bowing deeply but staring at the grime and blood on his sleeve when they thought he wouldn't notice.

He could feel more than see Ben being dragged along behind and grilled for information. James groaned internally—and maybe a little externally too—as he was whisked through the palace halls. One of the guards broke from the group and hurried up the grand staircase, no doubt to inform the King and Queen.

Great. Spectacular, even.

They reached Lady Anne's chamber within moments. The healer's room was tucked between the royal library and the south tower, a place that always smelled faintly of flowers and antiseptic. Floor-to-ceiling shelves of jars lined the walls, each labeled in her neat handwriting. A pointed window poured golden sunlight into the room and dust particles drifted lazily. A green fire burned beneath a hanging cauldron, and somewhere under it all lay the comforting scent of lavender soap.

The guards deposited both boys onto a cushioned bench before locking the door from the outside. The metallic click echoed louder than it should have. Ben slumped beside him, muttering about how this was "such a drag," and for once, James didn't argue. They sat in an oppressive silence that got louder as time went on. Despite the crushing weight of the stillness, James dared not disturb it. He only stared at his hand.

The rune gleamed faintly under the firelight—black and elegant, its edges forming loops and lines that pulsed as though alive. When he brushed his thumb across it, warmth surged up his arm, followed by a numb chill. It wasn't pain, exactly. It was worse: a feeling that something inside him was watching back.

He lost track of time until the healer herself swept inside, slamming the door and relocking it behind her.

Lady Anne turned, skirts rustling as she immediately started examining him. "Well, you two are a sight," she said, half exasperation, half genuine concern. A hand to his forehead, fingers on his pulse, light green eyes staring intently into his eyes. "I leave you alone for one morning—"

Ben shifted uncomfortably on the bench beside James. Obviously, the seriousness everyone was treating the situation with was doing nothing to ease his anxiety.

Her touch was gentle, but her energy was sharp and precise, like a blade. It was easy to see where Sarah got her discipline. James tried to sit straighter, which only made his arm ache more.

"Let's see the damage," she said briskly, taking his hands. When she turned his right palm upward, the color drained from her face. For a woman who had healed battlefield wounds, that alone was enough to make James's stomach drop.

She touched the rune lightly with the tip of one finger. A pulse of pain shot up his arm, bright and electric. He hissed, trying to pull away, but she held firm.

"James, what have you gotten yourself into this time?" she said, barely above a whisper.

Her voice wasn't scolding—it was the sound of someone realizing a problem had no easy cure. She released his hand, composed herself, and opened the door. "Fetch the King. And tell him to bring Lord Xavier. Immediately."

The guard bowed and bolted. The room seemed to shrink after he left.

Anne's composure cracked only once—a soft exhale, almost a sigh. Then she was moving again, flitting around the room, grabbing and mixing ingredients in a crystal bowl, all the while muttering under her breath about foolishness and *I don't know what you were thinking*. Every few seconds, she glanced at James, her jaw tight.

Ben fidgeted on his stool. "Should I... do something?"

"Yes," she said dryly, pouring powder into the bowl. "Drink this. Both of you."

Two vials appeared in her hands, dark liquid swirling inside. The smell alone was enough to make Ben grimace. "It looks like death."

"It'll taste worse," Anne said. "Drink."

James obeyed, coughing at the bitterness. The effects were immediate—his muscles relaxed, and the fire in his hand dulled to a faint hum. Even the cuts on his skin began to fade. Ben swallowed his with a muttered prayer and nearly gagged.

"Lovely," he said hoarsely. "Really delicious. Tastes like regret."

Before James could laugh, the door burst open again.

The King and Queen of Valenor swept in like a storm. King Alfred's golden hair caught the light in a way that always made James feel smaller. His mother, Queen Aria, was at his side—her lavender eyes wide, her voice trembling.

"James!"

He barely had time to brace before she threw her arms around him.

"I'm fine, Mother," he mumbled, voice muffled in her shoulder. "Really. Just a scratch."

"A scratch?" She pulled back, inspecting him head to toe, horrified. "You were found in the city covered in blood!"

Alfred's silence weighed heavier than her worry. He stepped forward, studying his son with an unreadable expression. He put his hand on his son's shoulder and gave it a squeeze, his face serious. Then his gaze shifted to James's hand.

"Show me."

James obeyed. The King's jaw tightened.

Lord Xavier entered behind them, his dark cloak whispering across the floor. His presence filled the room even before he spoke—a tall man with hair black as crows' wings and one eye veiled by a faint scar. His other eye, an unnatural silver, gleamed with restrained magic.

He crossed to James in two long strides, taking his hand without a word. The room held its breath as he examined the mark. When he finally looked up, his voice was quiet.

"This is no common curse."

Alfred's hand clenched on James's shoulder. "Is it one of Radha's?" he demanded.

"No," Xavier said. "Nor any I've seen before." He turned the boy's wrist gently, studying the veins beneath the skin. "But its power is old. Ancient. It's alive. As to its purpose, I think we will know more once James tells us what happened."

All eyes fell on James. He squirmed under the weight of their undivided attention, but he obeyed. He recounted everything that he and Ben had experienced, except admitting that he needed the ingredients for mischief. From their looks, he could tell they already knew. When he had finished, Xavier nodded thoughtfully.

"If it was indeed Sahir, then we can assume the curse is arcane in nature and powerful. It will take time to break."

"But you can break it?" Alfred asked, not bothering to hide his anxiety.

Xavier hesitated. "I'm not sure," he admitted.

Alfred's jaw clenched and the hand on James's shoulder tightened until he winced.

"There has to be a way," Alfred ground out through his teeth.

"Calm yourself, Alfred. There is no reason to panic yet. A curse this powerful will take time to mature. In the meantime, I can think of many places I can start, but it will require that I leave tomorrow."

"Do what you must," Alfred stated.

Xavier nodded and, with a sweep of his heavy traveling cloak, he was through the door.

James stared after him. Then he felt something inside snap. He stood, shrugging hands off and hurried to follow.

"Uncle Xavier! Let me come with you."

The words hung in the air like a challenge. The dark mage stopped, half-turned, and regarded him over one shoulder.

"You are not ready."

"Why not?!" James exploded, all his pent-up frustrations escaping in that one complaint. "I know you know what my teachers are saying. There is nothing more I can learn here. Please! Take me with you!"

Something that looked remarkably like a shadow of pity crossed Lord Xavier's stern face, but James blinked and it was gone.

"The places I am going are too dangerous for you as you are now. I cannot take you." James continued to stare defiantly back at Xavier, but he continued, "However, I do believe you are correct. We have some flexibility with time. I will stay through tomorrow night. I will train you personally until then."

"Yeah? You mean it?!" James asked, his face lighting up with excitement.

"First things first."

The King's voice startled him. He jumped and turned to face his father, who put a hand back on his shoulder and gave him a stern look.

"Let Anne finish examining you, then it's upstairs to get cleaned up."

James started to glare at his father out of habit, then thought better of it. It was best to keep him happy if it meant he could train with the dark mage.

James nodded instead, though the corner of his mouth betrayed a small, victorious smile. He looked back toward Xavier, who was already disappearing down the corridor, cloak trailing like shadow. The man didn't look back—but James swore he saw a faint smirk before the darkness swallowed him.

James allowed his father to steer him back towards Anne's chamber. They were met with Anne, who was ushering Ben out the door.

"They are going to be fine, Alfred," Lady Anne assured the King. "Aside from the curse, their injuries were mild. The medicine I gave them should be all they need, but I would like to examine them again in a day or two, just to be safe."

Alfred nodded at her, then turned to the boys.

"Okay, then go upstairs, both of you, and get cleaned up. You can join Xavier when you are done."

James nodded, Ben bowed, and the two hurried off towards their respective rooms.

James was loath to admit it, but he was glad to be home. The feeling swept over him as he closed his bedroom door behind him. He leaned heavily against it and slid to a sitting position on the floor, relaxing for the first time since it happened. He sighed deeply and rubbed his face with both hands. Then he held out his right hand and examined the mark again.

It looked almost innocent, like an old and slightly faded tattoo he'd had for years. He carefully ran his fingers over it, but this time there was no jolt of pain. Sahir's spell still rang in his ears. *Your talent will be your undoing.* Just what did that mean? He had never heard a spell like it before. He racked his brain trying to make sense of it all but kept coming up with nothing. He pulled his hair with a frustrated growl and gave up for the time being.

He dragged himself to his feet and examined his body in the full-length mirror. He did look bad. Anne's powerful medicine had healed his cuts and burns, but the evidence of damage was still obvious.

His usually shining gold hair was dull, disheveled, and dusty to the point of almost being brown. His face was covered in fine dust and mud was smeared across his cheek. His lips were chapped and dried blood clung to the center of his bottom lip and the corner of his mouth. His right arm was hairless to the elbow and streaked with soot. His pants were filthy and caked in mud. His shirt was little more than a rag; the tatters of what was left of the right sleeve clung pathetically to the shoulder. It was a shame. This had been his favorite shirt.

He peeled off the corpse of his top and allowed it to drop to the floor. He bent to remove his shoes but paused. He felt something in his pocket that hadn't been there in the morning.

Frowning, he reached in—and froze.

Two small leather pouches.

The contents of one shimmered faintly with powdered basilisk scales. The other glowed with the faint light of a wind crystal.

He stared at them, heartbeat quickening. Sahir had given him what he asked for. Despite everything—the curse, the pain, the disappearance—he had delivered.

The realization chilled him. Was that the "gift"? Or the first step in something worse?

James dropped both pouches on the floor beside his ruined clothes and stepped into the bath as the water began to steam. The heat hit him like a blessing. For a moment, the world shrank to soap, warmth, and the steady rhythm of his own breathing.

But the mark on his palm pulsed once—then again—like a heartbeat that wasn't his own.

He sank lower in the water, eyes closing.

Later, he would train.

Tomorrow, he would understand.

CHAPTER 4
SARAH THE FIRE MAGE

It's amazing how a bath can make a person feel like new. Clean, refreshed, and smelling faintly of cedar and rose oil, James felt almost human again—well, half-human. The steam had cleared his head and scrubbed the morning's chaos from his bones. Dressed in a soft linen shirt and fitted black trousers, he practically floated through his room, grinning at the thought that Lord Xavier—*Lord Xavier*—had agreed to train him personally. For once, luck seemed to be on his side.

He pulled open his door—and came almost nose to nose with the stern figure of Sarah.

Fuck, his luck had just run out.

She stood squarely in the doorway, blocking his path with military precision. She wore her usual floor-length crimson robes trimmed with gold flame embroidery, arms crossed like twin barriers. Her crimson-painted nails gleamed in the light as dangerously as her onyx eyes beneath the shadow of her famous hat. Tall, pointed, and broad-brimmed, it tilted slightly to one side in permanent defiance of gravity—its faded gray-black fabric patched near the base by a clumsy square of mismatched fabric and thread.

The patch, James knew all too well, was his fault.

The hat had been a gift from her father, Xavier himself, carried home from some foreign kingdom. Once, it had been as black as midnight. Then a certain over-eager prince had misfired a lightning spell near her workspace. The resulting hole had nearly ended their friendship. She'd refused every offer to have it repaired by palace tailors and had stitched it herself. The result wasn't pretty—but Sarah wore it like armor, a reminder that she fixed what others broke.

"Hello, Sarah," James said, every syllable dripping with exaggerated politeness. "To what do I owe the pleasure?"

Her eyes narrowed to slits. "What's this I hear about you getting yourself cursed?"

James leaned against the doorframe with his most infuriating grin. "I dunno. Shit happens?"

She exhaled through her nose, halfway between a sigh and the warning hiss of an oncoming fireball. "How many times do I have to tell you? Your actions are unbecoming of a future king—"

"If you want the job, you can have it!" The words were sharper than he intended. He shouldered past her and stormed down the corridor, boots echoing against marble.

For a heartbeat, silence followed—then the sound of quick footsteps as she caught up.

"You don't really mean that," she said, voice softer now but still edged.

"Don't I?" he muttered.

Being heir to Valenor's golden throne had never felt like a gift. Half-human, half-elf—he was a constant reminder of two worlds that only barely fit together. His father's ambition ran through the kingdom like iron; his mother's grace filled every quiet corner. Somewhere between them, he was supposed to be perfect.

Sarah said nothing for a while, maybe realizing he didn't want to talk. But restraint was never her strong suit.

"It isn't fair," she grumbled finally. "Why do you get to train with Papa?"

"Don't complain! He's your dad!" James shot back, some of his mischief returning. "And this is the first time he's agreed to train me, so don't ruin this for me."

That did it. Her temper sparked, and they bickered the rest of the way to the training grounds—at least until Xavier's dark silhouette appeared ahead. His single withering glance was enough to silence both of them instantly.

To James's mild horror, Sarah didn't leave. She folded herself cross-legged on the stone bench, chin propped on her fist, clearly determined to supervise. James ignored her as best he could and threw himself into training.

Lord Xavier was as precise and merciless as the rumors claimed. His movements were poetry sharpened into steel. James followed every motion, every incantation, every correction as though memorizing scripture. For the first time in what seemed like years, he felt like he was doing something that mattered.

By the time dusk streaked the courtyard, Ben had arrived. The fresh red handprint on his cheek said everything about how his afternoon with Lady Simone had gone. He winced when Sarah's gaze flicked toward it, but she mercifully stayed silent.

Finally, Xavier lowered his blade. "That's enough," he said simply. "Go. Eat. Rest."

"But Uncle Xavier," James started, panting. "Just one more—"

The man's single raised brow cut him off. James bit his tongue.

"Come back tomorrow morning," Xavier added, turning away. "We have time before the festivities begin."

"Yes!" James pumped his fist like a child who'd won a prize. Sarah's scowl could have melted steel.

"Sarah. Come with me," her father said, never looking back.

She threw James one last poisonous glare and followed.

James grinned after her, watching the two mages disappear into the dusk. Despite her temper, he was genuinely happy she'd get a rare evening with her father. Then he jogged to catch up with Ben.

They walked the long path back in companionable silence until the quiet got unbearable.

"So," James said, smirking sideways, "I see your meeting with Lady Simone went well."

Ben groaned. "Shut up. I don't want to talk about it."

James eyed the fading mark on his friend's olive skin and wisely dropped the subject. After a few minutes, he tried again, softer this time. "Hey. Thanks… for earlier. For helping me." Ben gave him a sideways look. James held it.

Eventually, Ben shrugged. "Don't mention it. Don't get all sappy—it's weird." He punched James's shoulder lightly, and just like that, the tension cracked.

James laughed. "Fair enough."

"Too bad you didn't get your ingredients," Ben said.

"Oh! Funny thing," James said, brightening. "I found them in my pocket. The crazy bastard actually gave them to me."

Ben froze. "You're not going to use them, right?"

James hesitated. "Maybe. It would be a shame to waste such good materials…"

"James, he cursed you!"

"Fine, fine." He sighed dramatically. "I'll behave."

Ben's dubious glance said he didn't believe a word of it.

Dinner that evening was stiff and miserable. His father was stern and distant, his mother serene but tight-lipped. His little sister, Heather, fidgeted beside her dessert spoon, the young princess not yet old enough to understand the atmosphere but wise enough not to speak. Lady Simone glared daggers at Ben; Lord George sat beside his son and pretended his soup was fascinating. Sarah looked like she was calculating how best to set James on fire without alarming the servants.

It wasn't long before his appetite vanished. He set down his fork and muttered a polite excuse before slipping away.

Back in his room, James flopped onto his bed, staring at the carved beams overhead. The day had been a disaster—and yet, somehow, not entirely hopeless. His training had been incredible. He could still feel the echo of Xavier's magic crackling in his veins.

He turned his right hand over in the lamplight. The rune gleamed faintly, almost innocent.

Your talent will be your undoing.

He traced the mark with one finger. It pulsed once, like a heartbeat.

"Great," he muttered, naturally turning to sarcasm to cover his worry. "That's reassuring."

A soft knock interrupted his thoughts. The door opened before he could answer.

His mother stepped in, elegant as moonlight, still in her fuchsia gown from dinner. Her silver hair—an inheritance from her elven line—glimmered against her warm pink skin.

"Hey," she said warmly.

"Hey, Mom," he said, wary. "What's up?"

"Excited for your big day tomorrow?"

"I guess," he admitted. "Mostly just… ready."

She smiled knowingly and sat on the edge of his bed. "Tomorrow, you'll be of age to rule." Her tone carried the weight of both pride and warning. "Your father and I were wondering…" she began delicately, "…if you've thought at all about how you feel about Sarah."

"What?!" He nearly choked. "Why would you want to know that?!"

"Well, being of age to rule also means that you are eligible to marry," she said patiently. "If you're interested in her, tomorrow might be a perfect opportunity to announce your intentions."

"I have *no* intentions!" he burst out. "She doesn't like me that way, and I sure as hell don't—wait, doesn't she get a say?!"

"Of course," Aria said quickly. "We'd never force you. We only thought—"

"I'm not interested in anyone!" he insisted, face hot.

Her expression softened, serene and far too knowing. "It's time to think about the future, James. The people need to see stability."

He groaned. "So you want me to announce I'm shopping for a spouse?"

She hesitated, then said innocently, "If not Sarah… is there someone else you're interested in? Benjamin, perhaps?"

James's face went crimson so fast it made his pointed ears glow. "Mom! What—no!" His words tripped over themselves. "He's—he's my *friend!*"

She laughed softly, the sound musical and maddening. "Elves don't see things as rigidly as humans, my love. Love takes many shapes."

"Yeah, well, humans gossip," he muttered, covering his burning face with his hands.

Her laughter softened to a fond smile. "Then perhaps no one, for now," she said gently. "But the people must see that their future king is building a lineage of his own. If you're not ready to choose, at least announce that you're open to finding a partner."

He sighed, staring at the ceiling again. "Fine."

She leaned down, kissed his forehead, and brushed a stray lock of gold hair aside. "Thank you, my son. I love you."

"I love you too, Mom," he mumbled, still mortified.

When she left, the room felt heavier.

Ben was right. This was a drag.

The next morning came too quickly. Training with Xavier was the only part that felt real. He poured himself into every motion until his sword felt like an extension of his arm—and his right arm felt like fire. By the end, he could barely hold the hilt. Xavier noticed, of course, but said nothing. That silence was worse than any reprimand.

The rest of the day blurred—crowds, music, smiling strangers, ceremonial gestures. He wore his gold circlet and his best clothes, posed for portraits, toasted dignitaries, and laughed at jokes he didn't hear. Ben hovered at his shoulder, concerned. James only smiled and said he was fine.

Dinner was the breaking point. When the King announced that his son was now "seeking a partner," something in James cracked. The hall erupted with cheers, the celebrations began anew. All he heard was the cage closing.

He stood, muttered some excuse, and turned to leave. He could feel Ben reaching out to stop him. He avoided his grasp and left without looking back.

He felt strange when he entered his room. As if he were in a trance, he stripped off the royal finery and pulled on a black traveling shirt with rose-pink trim, his light cloak, boots, and sword belt with his favorite hunting knife. His movements were automatic but sure. He packed coin, rations, and—after a pause—the small pouches from Sahir. He could still feel the mark throbbing in his palm.

He laced his traveling boots, then cracked his door and peered into the hallway. Deserted.

He crept to the armory and retrieved his best sword—a masterwork from the city of Laharas, the famed city of smiths and fire. *"Laharas iron never rusts," Ben said, running his finger along the blade. "I heard they quench it in dragon flame."* The old memory surfaced as he strapped it securely to his back and made his way to the gates. He could only pray Ben was right.

The fireworks for his birthday sat ready by the courtyard. For a fleeting moment, he considered dumping the basilisk powder into the barrels just to watch the sky burn.

Instead, he smirked.

Maybe next year.

Pulling his hood low, the half-elf prince slipped through the quiet halls toward the city gates.

The Hero King's heir was gone before the first firework touched the sky.

CHAPTER 5
LUSIN,
SON OF THE SERPENT KING

Lusin basked lazily on his favorite rock, staring up at the starry sky as he awaited the dawn.

There was no shortage of red sandstone outcroppings scattered throughout the Wastes—broken ribs of the earth thrust upward, sun-scorched and wind-smoothed. But this one had always belonged to him. It sat near enough to the lair to be convenient, just far enough to feel like freedom. A shallow dip had formed in its center over years of use, a perfect cradle for his spine. The graininess of the stone was just rough enough to help shed molting skin. It was comfort shaped from erosion and memory.

He did not have to wait long before dawn broke—a molten edge of gold splitting the horizon. The first slice of sunlight rose from the Great Sea and spilled over the cracked desert floor. The waves caught the light and threw it back like shattered mirrors. Lusin's skin warmed under the glow, easing joints stiff from the predawn chill. He inhaled deeply, letting the salt-and-sun-soaked breeze feather through his silver-blue hair, savoring the feeling of newness that every sunrise offered.

He plucked the last stubborn bit of molt from the back of his hand with absent-minded precision, then gently scratched the scales present only on the left side of his cheek and neck. The shed was nearly complete. Soon, he would leave again, and that thought brought a ripple of excitement through him. His shed had been unusually long this cycle, and he was eager to resume his quest for his Sun.

He lifted his chin, staring into the rising light. The sun painted his irises gold and set every scale under his eye shimmering like mother-of-pearl. He adored the sun, in all its forms—but sunrise was his favorite. The dawn didn't just warm his snow-white skin. It soothed something deeper, an ache behind his ribs that stiffened whenever he stayed underground for too long. The warmth seeped into bone and blood and memory. It reminded him that the world could still be gentle.

Tehi never understood this love of the sun. Not really. But Tehi loved him fiercely, and that was reason enough for tolerance. Still, Lusin knew that his brother was never far— nor was Nix, the poor water mage trapped forever in the role of reluctant nursemaid.

Lusin smiled to himself and stretched across the stone, limbs long and languid. Of course Nix was out there somewhere, sighing in the shadows.

As if summoned by the thought, a flicker of movement tugged at Lusin's attention. His brother's presence pressed like a change in air pressure.

"Lusin! You need to come in now!"

Lusin turned, unbothered, letting the sun continue to kiss his back. Tehi stood a short distance away, arms folded, posture rigid as ever. The scales that covered most of Tehi's body glinted under the morning light, each one steel-grey and edged like metal. His armor—leather reinforced with plates of silvered black—made him look like a war idol carved from dark marble.

Lusin, by contrast, looked like a dream. He wore his usual flowing silk tunic, white and weightless, tied with a sky-blue sash that fluttered around his hips in the breeze. The contrast between them—a storm and a sky—made him nearly laugh aloud. Instead, he softened the moment with a tilt of his head and a placid smile.

Tehi did not return it, but his eyes flickered with relief all the same.

Lusin rose smoothly—an elegant unwinding of limbs—and stepped lightly across the rough desert pavement toward the cave entrance. As he approached, a ripple of water manifested in the shadows ahead, resolving into the slim figure of Nix. The water mage waved cheerfully, then slipped into the darkness with the fluid ease of a fish diving into deep water.

Lusin chuckled. No matter how many times he saw Nix move like that, it still felt like watching water learn to walk.

Most would never guess, watching him, that Nix was the only one among them who wasn't a basilisk at all.

Long before Lusin's hatching, Nix had become a companion to the Serpent King. No one—not even Tehi—knew how it had happened. It was widely agreed, however, that trying to predict Radha's whims was like trying to predict the tides by staring at a single wave. Nevertheless, the old king had trusted Nix so deeply that he placed his own children in the water mage's care. He had been with them since the moment they had each cracked their shells.

Even now, Lusin could recall the first stories as Nix told them—how Radha's first son had come into the world with flaws that nearly killed him. Tehi's premature aging, his fragile bones, the strange instability of his internal magic—all of it should have ended him before he saw his first molt. It was only through Nix's constant vigilance that Tehi had survived at all.

Radha loved his firstborn deeply. But he had still longed—quietly, dangerously—for a son who was perfect.

Nine years later, Lusin was hatched.

That memory, though not his own, echoed through him sometimes. A reminder that he was not simply loved—he was hope incarnate. That was the weight Radha had given him at birth. A weight he carried still.

Now, grown, Lusin found himself increasingly haunted by the memory of simpler days. Times when he trained under Nix in the cool underground rivers, then climbed his favorite rocks to watch the stars unchallenged. Those nights felt impossibly far away now, swallowed by time and expectation.

He had mastered wind and lightning magic before his tenth hatching day, and his father's pride had been palpable. His basilisk gifts had manifested early and brutally. Where most of his kind could kill one creature with a glance, Lusin's gaze could kill entire crowds—mercilessly, instantly, and without distinction. A terrible gift. A miraculous weapon. A curse, if misused.

By sixteen, the Serpent King had decided. The quest would begin.

The search for his Sun.

Radha had spoken of it often but never fully explained it. His Sun was someone who would keep him from falling into the same darkness that Radha had nearly drowned in. A partner. A mirror. A necessary warmth against the creeping cold in his bones.

The idea fascinated him. Who were they? What would they feel like? Would their presence be as soft as the dawn or would it scorch, like the ferocity of the summer's noon on the desert sands?

He still didn't know. But the ache inside him—the cold coil tightening around his heart—told him that finding them was not optional.

He had traveled through forests and mountains and drowned cities. He had met beautiful strangers and courted them briefly, only to feel disappointment hollow him out every time. No matter how kind or clever or striking they were, their presence always left him cold.

Lusin had learned early that mortals were loudest just before they became dangerous.

At first, he had dealt with such inconveniences without much thought. A glance held a moment too long. A gaze met and not broken. Noise giving way to silence, quick and final.

It had not troubled him. The dead were not his concern, and the living rarely lasted long enough to become one.

Only later did he notice the pattern it left behind.

Keeping his heritage secret—or at least less obvious—always became more difficult during his molt. Scales peeling, magic unstable, emotions raw—the shedding made disguise impossible. He usually retreated to the wilderness, but this time the proximity to home tempted him. Tehi had nearly burst from joy when he arrived. Lusin had pretended not to notice how his brother's voice shook.

Lusin had learned that his brother's overprotective tendencies were not entirely unwarranted. Hunters found him from time to time. They always did, eventually—drawn by rumor, by fear, by the quiet confidence of men who believed themselves prepared.

He no longer remembered their faces. Only the brief irritation of interruption, and the longer inconvenience of what followed if he left too many questions unanswered behind him.

Now, his shed was ending, and the familiar rhythm of travel tugged at him again.

He reached Tehi at last. His brother's arms were folded, brow furrowed—not angry, just concerned. Always concerned.

Lusin smiled—not the cunning smile he wore in taverns and cities, but the quiet, genuine one reserved for his brother. Tehi didn't smile back, but his posture eased just enough to reveal affection beneath the scowl.

"Hello, brother," Lusin said, and wrapped him in an embrace without warning.

Tehi returned the gesture stiffly, like a man trying to hug a thunderclap. And yet—he did return it.

They separated, and Tehi met his gaze with stern eyes.

"Father wishes to see you."

Lusin inclined his head. "Yes, I will go immediately."

He left without looking back. The sun pressed at his spine as though reluctant to release him, but the cave welcomed him home with cool, familiar breath. Pale braids of mineral threaded through the stone like veins. Pools reflected faint light like trapped starlight. The scent of ancient water and crushed herbs lingered in the air.

He needed no torch. He could walk every passage blindfolded.

But he liked seeing them—the patterns in the stone, the folded layers of time. He loved home, truly. He simply wished it did not hurt to remain here.

Radha was exactly where Lusin expected him to be.

"My dear Lussssin," Radha hissed warmly, his thin lipped smile stretching just a touch too wide.

"Hello, Father," Lusin replied, voice even and gentle.

Radha stepped close, one clawed hand resting on Lusin's shoulder, the other threading through his hair. The gesture should have looked violent. Instead, it was tender—almost motherly. In other lands, the gesture would be strange. Here, it was home.

"Lusssssin, how hasss the quest for your Sun progressed?"

The question was expected, yet still carried pressure like a crushing tide.

"It has been… unsuccessful."

He hated the sound of it. As if failure were a confession.

Radha's expression did not break. His eyes—serpent-yellow and ancient—softened, but only barely. A brief touch to Lusin's hair, a pat on his shoulder. A wordless acknowledgment of defeat.

"This news iss… troubling, although it iss not unexpected."

Silence built, oppressive and cold.

"Father?" Lusin asked at last, voice small despite himself. "I have been searching for four years now. This search is starting to feel hopeless."

Radha turned, spine stiff as a spear. "The lack of progress iss disappointing, but you musst not give up, my son." His gaze sharpened, voice coiling with command. "It iss imperative that you succeed. You musst find your Sun."

Lusin bowed his head. The ache in his chest throbbed in agreement. He needed warmth. He needed something to banish the cold he carried. The urgency was real—and growing.

Then Radha asked, "Have you tried traveling towardss the capital?"

Lusin's head lifted. He had not.

He had avoided it deliberately.

The capital was crowded. Watched. Alive in a way that wilderness was not. He preferred the quiet. The birds. The streams. The open sky. He had learned quickly to hide his scales and temper his voice. A hood, long sleeves, and silence allowed him to pass as something strange but tolerable. A fae, perhaps. A traveler. Not a monster.

He had learned that it was easier to move through the world if he left fewer absences behind him.

Fewer silences where voices should have been.

Fewer questions that grew teeth.

Restraint, it turned out, was not kindness. It was efficiency.

But the capital… the capital would require something more. More disguise. More caution. More lies. More restraint.

His father had never rebuked him for the dead.

That, perhaps, had been the rebuke.

And yet—

If his Sun might be there, then the added risk hardly mattered.

"No, Father. I have not. I will leave immediately."

Radha nodded, slow and deliberate. "Good. You are my hope, Lussin. The light that will undo the darknesss that once claimed me. Go, and do not return until you have found what the heavensss owe you."

Those words—*light can burn as easily as it warms*—followed him out.

Tehi waited in the corridor like a sentinel.

"Well?" he asked.

"Father wishes me to travel toward the capital."

Tehi's jaw tightened, and his voice dropped into iron. "Then I'm going with you."

Lusin almost smiled. "No, Brother. You will stay here."

Tehi drew breath to argue—and stopped. One look at Lusin's eyes silenced him. For once, Lusin spoke with complete authority.

"I will be fine. You have spent too long worrying over me. Rest."

He touched Tehi's shoulder gently. The gesture seemed to both wound and ease him.

Lusin returned to his chambers in silence.

He stripped off his silk and replaced it with traveling clothes—soft boots, long sleeves, a hooded cloak. He adjusted the lines of fabric until it concealed the shimmer of his scales. He looked into the polished obsidian mirror and tilted his head. A stranger looked back.

He packed lightly. Water. Dried rations. His silver double-edged daggers wrapped in cloth. His father's sigil.

When he stepped outside again, twilight had bled to violet. The dunes in the west swallowed the remains of the glowing red sun. The wind carried the taste of salt and lightning.

Lusin paused and looked back only once. The lair—a carved mouth a the bluff nestled in sand—yawned in silence. It was his birthplace, his sanctuary… and his cage.

He turned west, following the disappearance of the beloved sun.

The ache in his chest grew brighter, sharper, purposeful.

Somewhere beyond the horizon waited his Sun—the one who could warm him, heal him, break him, or burn him alive.

The desert whispered around his boots.

He walked until the cave disappeared behind him.

He did not look back again.

CHAPTER 6
ONE STORMY NIGHT

It was raining.

Not the gentle kind that kissed the desert dust, but the heavy, relentless kind that made even the stones feel cold. The kind that carried weight in every drop—each impact a tiny drumbeat against roof and earth. Lusin didn't usually mind the rain; he'd walked through tempests fierce enough to strip bark from trees.

But tonight, the chill carried a bite that sank deeper than skin, weighing down his limbs, stiffening his joints, and tugging at old exhaustion. He suspected it was simply the weariness of yet another day with no Sun, no warmth, no progress—and that thought alone made the rain feel colder.

The tavern just outside the small town stood as a lone beacon against the cold. Its windows glowed gold, blurring behind streaks of rainwater, and plumes of smoke drifted from the stone chimney in lazy, curling ribbons.

Lusin stood at the threshold, his hood pulled low. Rain slid off the fabric like melting silver.

He stepped inside.

Warmth hit him like a spell. Heat kissed his soaked skin through the fabric of his clothes, and firelight flickered across dark wooden beams polished by years of use. The scent of roasted meat, spilled ale, damp cloaks, and pipe smoke saturated the air. It was, in the mortal sense, "cozy"—a word Lusin still wasn't entirely sure he understood, but he liked the way it felt.

He lingered by the entrance, letting his golden eyes adjust to the dimness. The lanterns burned low, their light hazy with smoke, turning everything amber and soft-edged. A few drinkers glanced up, curiosity flickering before dull indifference returned. Good. He preferred it that way. In a place where drunks bickered and minstrels strummed out-of-tune songs, another silent stranger hardly mattered.

The tavern was moderately crowded—travelers, laborers, merchants, the usual assortment of humans sprinkled with a handful of other races, running from the weather or from their own thoughts. He approached the bar.

"A mead and a room," he said, setting down a heavy gold coin—more than enough to cover drink, bed, and the unspoken request for privacy.

The innkeeper studied him briefly, eyes flicking across his shrouded features, but said nothing. Only a well-practiced nod as he swept the coin away and replaced it with a bronze key and a full glass of mead.

Lusin didn't actually care for mead. It was too sweet, too thick. But he had long ago found that tavern patrons trusted men who drank. A cup in hand provided cover. Drinking gave him an excuse to sit still and observe.

The booth he chose was tucked into a shadowed corner beside a fogged window. A small gas lamp burned above, painting the wood table in honeyed hues. He set the drink before him and leaned back, letting the steady hum of the room wash over him. Condensation dripped down the glass in lazy rivers, catching the light like faint silver threads.

Lusin's gaze drifted to the reflection on the table's surface. His own face looked back—pale skin touched faintly with shimmer, eyes bright and unblinking, a few scales catching the lamplight like pearls beneath water. He traced a droplet of condensation with one finger until it merged into the puddle near his glass. The motion was small, repetitive, soothing.

He took a sip of the mead, tolerating its unpleasant taste and texture, and let his eyes wander across the room. People-watching had long served as both amusement and survival tactic. Studying faces, mannerisms, postures—it let him separate danger from disinterest long before threats became real. It helped him understand the world without needing to participate in it. And sometimes, rarely, it made him forget he was alone.

Tonight, however, the room was dull. Drunks flirted with serving girls. A trio of thugs played dice with the kind of laughter that usually led to bruises. A bard with a cracked lute tried to sing over the noise. Nothing caught his interest. Nothing deserved the effort of engagement.

He considered retiring early, perhaps rereading the old book he carried in his pack, or simply listening to the storm from the quiet of his rented room.

And then—

The door opened.

The wind rushed in first, scattering loose parchment and extinguishing two candles. Rain followed, glittering in the lamplight. But none of that mattered compared to the figure framed in the doorway.

Lusin froze.

A young man stood there—just a silhouette against the storm at first, but as he stepped past the threshold, warmth struck like dawn. His clothes were soaked, but even drenched they shone rich, tailored, unmistakably expensive. His hair, damp gold, clung in graceful waves around his face, each strand reflecting the light like threads pulled from the sun itself. His skin was warm-toned, paler than desert sand and darker than snow, and his ears were delicately pointed—half-elf.

And then he looked up.

His eyes were blue. Not just blue—turquoise, bright and clear and impossibly alive. They were like a cloudless sky on a summer afternoon. Like the heart of the sea under full sunlight.

Like everything Lusin had been searching for.

Lusin forgot to breathe.

It felt as if the world had been locked in shadow for years and someone had finally cracked open the horizon. Warmth bloomed through his chest, spreading from his heart outward, easing a cold he had never fully acknowledged. His pulse quickened—not with hunger or threat, but with recognition.

So this was what it felt like to find the Sun.

And now that he had found it, he knew with terrifying certainty—he would never be able to let it go.

His mind whispered it, certain before logic could catch up.

And he wasn't the only one who noticed him.

The thugs Lusin had ignored earlier began to stir. Eyes locked onto the newcomer like vultures spotting carrion… or treasure. The biggest one, thick-shouldered and leering, nudged his companions with a grin. The scent of wealth—and assumed weakness—had reached them.

Lusin watched.

The golden boy brushed rain from his shoulders, attempting to compose himself, but the moment he straightened, the thugs descended. They boxed him in, forcing him against the bar.

"Hey, pretty boy," the biggest one sneered, words slurred with drink. "Have a drink with us." The young man's face twisted with disgust.

Lusin didn't need to hear the tone. He could read it in their posture, in the way their eyes narrowed not with attraction but possession. The beautiful stranger tried to step away, but hands pushed him down onto a stool. Fingers slid across his coat, his hair, his sleeve—filthy hands on sunlight.

Something inside Lusin snapped.

Not rage—not exactly. Something deeper. Primal. Sacred.

How dare they.

The heat that bloomed in him was not wrath but instinct—a fierce, unmistakable certainty. The Sun did not belong here. Not among grime and greasy hands and hungry eyes. He did not belong anywhere near danger. He was a treasure, a dawn, a miracle.

And no one would touch him while Lusin still drew breath.

He moved.

Not hurriedly—gliding. Silent. Intention sharp as a knife. His shadow passed between tables unnoticed until he stood within striking distance.

The thugs did not notice. The beautiful man tried to stand but he was shoved down again. The thugs laughed and jeered. He went for his knife but his blue gaze scanned the room and his fingers fell away from the leather hilt.

Then, the largest thug punched the beautiful man in the face. That was enough.

Silver flashed.

Three of them fell before they even realized a threat existed—precise slashes along arms, legs, nothing lethal but enough to drop them screaming. A table toppled over with the force of their collapse.

Now the room noticed.

Gasps, shouts. Chairs scraped. The music stopped. The tavern's atmosphere changed from dull chaos to watchful, anxious.

The remaining thugs backed away from Lusin, eyes wide, scrambling over each other. He was no longer simply a stranger.

He was a predator.

Another lunged. Lusin parried easily, twisting past the blade with sinuous grace before disarming the man and sending him crashing into a wall. But in the struggle, a hand caught the edge of his hood—

—and tore it away.

Gasps erupted across the tavern.

His scales gleamed silver-blue in the firelight, scattered like jewels across his left cheek and down his jaw. His hair, soaked and pale, slid loose like a serpent's coil. And his eyes—golden, luminous, inhuman—shone with unmistakable basilisk power.

The room froze.

Someone screamed.

It broke the spell.

Lusin hissed a warning as he seized the golden man— gently, but securely—and fled. He crossed the tavern and bounded up the stairs in one surreal, fluid movement, no longer bothering to hide his identity. Recognition would provide protection tonight.

He was through the thick door of his rented room without pausing and disappeared into the darkness with his prize firmly in hand. The heavy door slammed behind them. Lusin locked it immediately. Even though he knew no one was foolish enough to follow a basilisk into its lair, he still desired to take precautions. Never before had he found himself in possession of something so precious.

He turned his attention back to the beautiful man and was surprised to find that he was struggling against him, breathing hard. Even now—frightened, dazed, trembling—he was stunning. His hair had fallen messily into his eyes. His breath shook.

Lusin loosened his grip and the man landed a solid kick to his chest, pushing him off completely. Once free, the man scrambled backwards attempting to make a frantic escape but his back collided hard with the bed and he tumbled to the rough wood floor. His weapons skittered away with loud metallic scattering.

The Sun scrambled up, disoriented but ready to fight, hand searching blindly for his knife and sword.

He can't see in the dark, Lusin realized.

Lusin moved quickly and caught the man's wrists, holding them without hurting him. The stranger struggled at first, muscles tense, breath ragged, all pride and fear and defiance. But when brute force failed, he froze—thinking, recalibrating.

"Who are you?!" he demanded. His voice cracked with adrenaline. "What do you want with me?!"

Lusin opened his mouth—and found he had no answer.

He had acted on instinct. Every decision had been a reaction to seeing him threatened. Now that they were alone, the part of his mind capable of reason stuttered and fell silent.

He only knew one truth:

He couldn't let him leave.

"If you're going to kill me," the man said, voice tight, "do it."

Lusin's grip loosened.

He had killed countless beings in his life. Even those who begged. Even those who couldn't fight back. But the thought of harming this one made him feel sick.

He answered instead, voice low. "My name is Lusin."

A breath of tension left the young man's body. Not trust—not yet—but curiosity.

The man hesitated. "…Ok, *Lusin,* what do you want with me?"

Lusin had no name for the feeling. No plan. No logic. Just an instinct sharp as hunger and deep as prayer.

He wanted to protect him.

He wanted to stay near him.

He wanted warmth.

He wanted… the Sun.

The man tore free and turned toward the door. If he truly chose to leave, Lusin knew he'd have to let him go.

"Please," Lusin said—desperately, helplessly—"don't go."

Something in his voice must have reached him. The man stopped, hand on the brass handle, not moving but he tilted an ear to show he was listening.

Lusin grasped for anything—any question that might keep him here.

"Why didn't you defend yourself?"

The stranger paused.

"…Don't you want to know my name first?"

"Yes." The answer was immediate. Honest. "I want to know everything about you."

The young man sighed, defeated in a small, strange way. "I suppose if you wanted to kill me, you would've already tried." Lusin nodded, forgetting for a moment that the man couldn't see him.

"If we're going to talk," he added weakly, "can we do it in the light?"

Lusin reached up and turned the gas lamp.

Light flooded the room.

And there he was—fully illuminated, fully breathtaking. His golden hair dried into soft waves. His eyes, now visible, shone with brighter blues than tropical seawater. His skin was warm, sun-kissed, alive.

For the first time in his life, Lusin understood what it meant for beauty to hurt.

"James," the stranger said quietly, refusing to meet his eyes. "My name is James. You gave me your name so it's only fair I give you mine." He said as he scratched the back of his head. His warm skin was growing pinker.

Lusin whispered it back like a prayer.

James.

"Why didn't you defend yourself? I could sense that they were no match for you."

"Oh, well… There wasn't enough room. I was afraid that I'd accidentally destroy the building if I acted. I have to ask, what's with the scales? Not that I don't like them, I've just never seen that before." James rambled gesturing towards his own cheek with a finger. His face was beet red from collar bone to the roots of his hair but Lusin couldn't fathom why.

"I'm a basilisk." Lusin replied simply. The effect on James was immediate. His eyes widened and he unconsciously took a half step back. His hand went for his knife again but this time Lusin didn't stop him. James's fingers fidgeted with the leather wrapped handle, then fell away as he released a shaky breath.

"Then if you had wanted to kill me, I'd be long dead by now. I guess that explains everyone's reactions downstairs when your hood came off. They knew, didn't they?" Lusin nodded. "Aren't you afraid they are going to, you know, follow you up here…?" James asked nervously, implying what he meant with a wave of his hand.

"They know what I am and they would never follow me to my lair. Undoubtedly, they believe I have taken you with the intention of eating you." James' eyes widened considerably as his explanation sank in. Again, he shifted towards the door. "But I have no wish to eat you." Lusin clarified. James visibly relaxed but didn't drop his guard completely.

Finally, James asked the question that mattered:

"Lusin… What *are* your intentions with me?"

The answer came without hesitation, honest and terrifying.

"I wish to protect you."

"Why?" James whispered. "You don't even know me."

Lusin met his eyes.

"I think… you are my Sun."

The words hung between them like a spell.

James's lips parted, his bright blue eyes wide. "Your…
Sun?" he echoed, disbelief threaded with something gentler.

Lusin nodded once. "The one I've been searching for."

Thunder murmured in the distance. Rain traced silver
lines down the glass, and for a heartbeat, neither spoke. James's
gaze lingered on him—half fear, half wonder—and in that
charged silence, something unseen began to turn, as slow as
a dawn breaking over the horizon.

CHAPTER 7
THE ROAD AND THE SUN

James lay in the dark, pretending to sleep while the faint lamplight traced rippling gold lines across the ceiling. Rain hissed softly on the windowpane, the sound waxing and waning with the wind as if the night itself were drawing long, steady breaths. The mattress gave beneath his shoulder blades with the particular sag of a bed that had seen a hundred travelers and held none of them for long. The room smelled faintly of damp wool, tallow smoke, and the ghost of old ale—banal comforts that felt almost luxurious after the last two days.

He couldn't close his eyes for more than a handful of heartbeats at a time. Even without looking, he could feel Lusin's attention on him: not invasive, exactly, but fixed—unblinking. The basilisk had taken up position beside the door and not moved since. James could sense him by the quiet pressure of his presence.

In less than forty-eight hours, he had fled the capital, weathered a storm, nearly mugged, and now found himself the semi-willing captive—guest?—of a basilisk who had calmly told him he was his Sun. The absurdity of it wanted to make him laugh out loud. He pressed the heel of his hand to his mouth and breathed through the urge.

Well. At least life wasn't boring.

They hadn't spoken much after that declaration. James had half-muttered a protest and half-yawned at the same time, and Lusin—voice gentle but impossible to argue with—had told him to rest. When James hesitated at the single bed, Lusin had offered a careful, awkward smile and said he would keep watch. It was an odd smile, not quite practiced, like a mask someone had only seen and never worn; on another person it might have been unsettling. On Lusin it turned disarming, as if he were trying very hard to translate a feeling into a human expression and hoping he'd gotten it right.

James lay very still under the scratchy, moth-eaten blanket. He tried to count his breaths. He tried to list the constellations in order. He tried to imagine what Sarah would say if she could see him now. (Something blistering, probably. Something correct.) Every few minutes he let himself glance at Lusin. In the dim, the basilisk's eyes were faintly luminous; the lamplight found the arcs of his scales, turning them into soft coins embedded in marble. He looked like a statue of something sacred left in a shrine—a creature carved to hold vigil and never tire of it.

James knew he shouldn't trust him. He'd been told his whole life to be wary of the Old Blood and anything that wore scales or bore fangs beneath a human smile. But the fear that training should have conjured refused to rise. Somewhere between the bar and Lusin presenting his name, something in him had simply decided: *this creature means you no harm.* It was patently illogical. It felt true anyway.

Still, his nerves wouldn't settle. Any minute, he kept thinking, the townsfolk would bring torches and pitchforks, as if outrage bred better courage than sense. He listened hard for shouts that never came. The storm wrote its soft script on the glass, the lamplight ebbed, and Lusin did not move.

When dawn finally pried at the edges of the cloud cover, the dark turned to a gentle pewter. James slipped from the bed with the affronted grace of a cat evicted from a warm patch of sun and pretended his joints didn't complain. He pushed his arms into his cloak and tied the throat with swift fingers. By the time he looked up, Lusin had already unbolted the door. Neither of them spoke. There was nothing to say that wouldn't feel as fragile as the hush itself.

They slipped through the abandoned tavern, past the cold hearth and chairs left where they had fallen, and out into the gray morning. The rain had settled into a fine mist that beaded on eyelashes and glassed their cloaks with tiny droplets. The street was mostly empty: a woman emptying wash water outside her hut, a cart creaking toward the square, a trio of ravens arguing over something unidentifiable near the trees' edge. The town wore last night's disorder with the indifference of places used to such things.

They walked side by side and apart, close enough for their sleeves to brush and far enough for either to pretend it was an accident. The rooftops around them hunched like wet beasts. Water dripped from eaves in steady, plucked notes. The smell of fresh bread escaped a bakery door as someone within cracked it open to bring in more wood; the scent, warm and yeasty, slid under James's ribs and reminded him he had not eaten since a handful of hours and a lifetime ago.

Lusin seemed immune. The basilisk walked with liquid economy, each step the same as the last, as if his body had been taught a single flawless motion and saw no reason to deviate. When he turned his head, scales along his jaw caught the thin light like frost. James tried not to stare and failed spectacularly.

He found himself cataloging details: the pattern of scales beneath Lusin's left eye; the way shoulder-length hair—if hair was the word—shimmered with the palest blue where it escaped the hood; the whisper-smooth movement of a sleeve when he lifted his hand; the way that white, not-quite-human skin reflected morning like porcelain. James's favorite feature by far were the scales.

He marveled at how smoothly and naturally they appeared from the skin. His eyes followed how they flowed around his jaw and down the side of his neck to blend back into skin at his slender collarbone, both only just visible through a gap in the folds of his hood. It made him curious if Lusin had other patches of scales elsewhere on his body.

Part of him wanted to reach out, to learn if those scales were glass-smooth or fine as sand. He pressed his mouth into a line and faced forward. Asking to touch a near-stranger—especially a one who had very recently abducted you to an inn room—seemed unwise.

Silence stretched. Even the mist seemed to hear it.

Eventually James decided that embarrassment was preferable to drowning in his own thoughts. "So… Lusin," he said, and only then remembered he had no follow-up prepared. Lusin turned his full attention on him, golden eyes bright as new coin. The words stripped out of James's head like threads from an old shirt.

"Uh—where are you from?" he blurted.

"The Basilisk Wastes," Lusin said, as if he were describing a street two blocks over. "I presume you're from the capital."

"What? Why would you think that?" James asked, his voice climbing higher than he'd intended.

Lusin's mouth did that almost-smile again. It was a small movement, restrained, but James felt the intent of it. "Your clothes," Lusin said. "No one here wears silk with gold trim. And your hair and eyes—rare colors. As far as I know, only the King and the Prince possess them."

James's foot missed half a step. He managed not to skid. He also managed, barely, not to slap both hands to his head like a child caught stealing tarts.

He knows.

Lusin did not press. He only kept walking, that faint not-quite-smile warming at the edges, eyes on the road.

James tried again some time later, when the dirt road leveled and the fog thinned enough that their exhalations were barely visible. "What brings you this far from the Wastes?" he asked, then winced internally at how clumsy it sounded, as if he were asking a stranger what business they had in his favorite chair.

"I've been traveling for years," Lusin said. "Searching for my Sun."

There it was again, that word like a bell rung in a distant room. It moved something under James's sternum he didn't have language for. He wanted to ask what exactly he meant by that but couldn't think of a way that wouldn't be rude. He was saved from deciding by Lusin's voice.

"What about you, Prince James?" the basilisk asked gently. "What are you doing outside the capital?"

James nearly tripped over a loose stone. He recovered inelegantly, arms pinwheeling once. "How did you—how do you know I'm the Prince?" he demanded, cheeks heating.

Another of those almost-smiles. "You confirmed it yourself just now."

James groaned, thoroughly. "Smooth," he muttered to himself. "Real smooth." He considered inventing a tale about secret missions and noble quests, then imagined Sarah appearing from the nearest doorway to pin him to the wall with a look. His stomach felt hollow and raw, a scraped place that had not healed since the mark burned into his palm. He found that palm with his other hand, rubbing the center with his thumb as if he could erase the memory with friction.

He stopped walking without realizing it and held his hand out. The rune lay black and perfect at the center of his palm, crisp lines and curves sunk into skin like ink poured into a cut. Mist slicked across it and beaded. He hated it. He feared it. He didn't know which was worse.

"It's this," he said. "It's a curse. No one knows anything about it. I left home in order to find a way to break it." The words sounded steadier in the air than they did in his head. Maybe because saying them made them feel like part of a story where things could be solved. "Problem is, I have no idea where to start."

Lusin's expression altered in a way James couldn't name—something like alertness braided with tenderness. He took James's hand between both of his, careful, deliberate. His fingers were cool, smooth, and strong. The pure white skin joined smoothly with scales covering the backs of his hands, each small plate laid neatly against the next. The touch stole James's breath in a way that had nothing to do with pain. Then Lusin's thumb brushed the mark.

Pain exploded up James's arm—hot, wrong, a nerve-line set ablaze. He hissed between his teeth and jerked back, every muscle tightening around the spark.

Lusin released him at once. "How long ago?" he asked. His voice held no panic, only compressed urgency.

"A couple of days," James managed. He braced his hands on his thighs and breathed until the ache receded to a bright throb. The skin around the rune seemed to pulse in time with his heartbeat, as if it now had one of its own.

"Do you know who did it?" Lusin asked.

"An arcane mage. Sahir." The name tasted like iron.

For an instant, something sharpened behind Lusin's eyes, as if a thought had flashed and been hidden again. "I do not know that name," he said. "But an arcane curse is powerful... and dangerous."

The understatement of the century. James swallowed. "Do you know how to lift it?"

"I do not," Lusin answered. He hesitated, then: "But my father might. His knowledge of dark and arcane magic is vast. If you wish, I can take you to him."

James blinked at him—at the simplicity of the offer, at the straightforward way hope sometimes dressed itself and stood in the road like a signpost you'd been too tired to lift your head and notice. "Really?"

Lusin inclined his head. "He lives in the Basilisk Wastes."

"Oh. Right." James found a shred of humor and held onto it. *Of course he does.* "Do you think he'll see me?"

"I have no doubt," Lusin said. He didn't say why. He didn't have to. The certainty in his voice did the work.

For the first time since he'd woken on that blasted and scorched patch of earth, something like excitement edged into his chest. It was small and stubborn and glittered like mica under dirt. He let himself look at it. He let himself believe it might grow.

"Okay," he said, surprising himself with the steadiness of it. "Let's go see your dad."

Lusin's answering grin was immediate and unguarded— the first expression James had seen on him that seemed to fit without translation. It softened his face and made the scales glow. It was like watching a full moon step from behind a cloud.

They pressed on, following a rutted road that unwound toward the low hills like a ribbon forgotten by a giant child. The mist lightened by degrees. Birds began in ones and twos, then in argument; a lark streaked from a hedgerow and vanished into the gray. The world around them carried that clean smell roads wear after rain: damp earth, bruised grass, the faint sharpness of crushed mint somewhere unseen.

James found his shoulders relaxing. The tension that had wound itself through his spine like wire since the tavern didn't loosen all at once, but it relented in inches. The road had always done this to him: smoothed him into himself, pared the day down to simple matters of horizon and pace. Even the throb in his palm seemed to accept the compromise and kept mostly quiet under his sleeve.

"Last night you didn't move," James said, glancing sideways as he broke the silence. "You were a statue."

"I was watching," Lusin replied, as if that were sufficient. Perhaps it was.

"For me?" The words came out before James could leash them.

"Yes," Lusin said simply.

Heat climbed the back of James's neck. He wanted to find it annoying. He did not. He searched for safer ground. "So. Wastes," he said. "What's it like?"

"Open," Lusin said after a moment's thought. "Red rock. Bright water in the Great Sea. Sand. Heat that both warms and sears. The horizon is honest there." His voice smoothed on the description into something close to longing.

James pictured it: a sky with enough room to think beneath; stones that took the sun like a blessing; a heat that seared away everything superfluous. He hadn't realized he missed the horizon until Lusin named it. The palace had its own grandeur, but its halls measured distance in staircases and obligations. The road drew a straight line across his mind and asked nothing more than that he follow it.

They stopped around midmorning—if the pale quality of the light could be called morning—under a twisted hawthorn that had decided the ditch was as good a home as any and grown accordingly.

A farmhouse squatted a field over, its low stone wall greened with moss. A woman with a scarf tied over her hair stood by a croft of beehives with a smoker. Bees lifted and resettled in gleaming clouds. Lusin waited beside the road while James crossed the muddy verge, hands open and visible. He traded coin for a small loaf and a jar of new honey. The woman pretended not to recognize him and did an admirable job.

They ate standing beneath the hawthorn. Lusin ate with the neat focus of someone for whom sustenance was more ritual than appetite. When a streak of honey glinted along his knuckle, he paused and regarded it as if deciding which common custom applied. James, who had solved the question by simply licking his own thumb clean, watched with naked interest.

Lusin lifted his hand and, solemn as a priest, pressed the joint of his thumb lightly to his tongue. James forgot to breathe for two seconds. He decided the mist was to blame.

They kept walking. The world lifted gradually around them into low, scrubby hills. Heather swept in patches like smoke. A shepherd appeared over a rise, his cloak oiled against the wet; his dog kept the edge of his flock in a perfect scalloped line as they poured across the track. The man touched two fingers to his brow as they passed. Lusin inclined his head. James did the same, remembering at the last instant to make it a stranger's nod rather than a prince's acknowledgment.

James's palm had begun to ache again, a dull pressure that sat under the skin as if someone were pressing a thumb there from the inside. He flexed his fingers, shook his wrist, tried to ignore it. He did not complain. He had decided that he would not give the curse more breath than it already stole. Lusin seemed to sense the tension without asking. Once, he slowed of his own accord as they descended a slope that was slick and deceptively steep, and James pretended not to notice that the pace change matched the rhythm of the pulse in his hand.

"Does it hurt now?" Lusin asked, eyes flicking once to James's sleeve.

"A little," James said, because for once the polite lie felt unnecessary between them.

James tried to picture the father Lusin had offered so casually—the one with vast knowledge and, presumably, opinions about princes with cursed hands. He tried to imagine arriving in a place called the Basilisk Wastes at the side of a creature who had dragged him up a staircase and then asked permission to stand guard over his sleep. He tried to reconcile the cardamom sweetness of the honey still clinging to the roof of his mouth with the iron taste that name—*Sahir*—left every time he said it.

He thought, too, of Sarah's hat, of the way it dipped slightly to one side where he had singed it years ago; of his mother's hand smoothing his hair when she thought he was out of breath from exertion rather than fear; of the King's jaw tightening when someone said the word *curse*. He thought of Ben's long-suffering sighs and the way laughter would escape him anyway.

He should feel guilt like a millstone. He should be pierced by the sharpness of leaving. He would be, later.

"You said 'Sun,'" James heard himself say quietly, as if testing the word in a new room.

Lusin's gaze slid to him. "Yes."

"What does it mean to you?" He wasn't sure he wanted the answer; he knew he did.

Lusin considered. "It means," he said slowly, "the center. The thing that makes everything else remember its orbit." He tilted his head, as if listening to a translation whispered in a different language. "Warmth that is not just heat. Light that makes more light."

James swallowed. "And you think that's me."

"I know it," Lusin said.

"I don't know what to do with that," he admitted, voice almost lost to the whisper of grass.

"You don't need to do anything with it," Lusin said. "It is not a task."

James let out a breath he hadn't realized he'd been holding. "That's new."

"Tasks come later," Lusin said, and there was the ghost of the not-quite-smile again.

The track turned toward the southeast in a slow curve. Somewhere beyond that bend, the land would begin, in small, almost invisible ways, to become the Wastes. James didn't know what that meant on a map. He knew only that it meant *forward*.

The curse pulsed once, hard and impatient under his skin, and he swallowed against the flare. He looked at Lusin. Lusin looked back. No words passed between them. None were needed.

They set their feet toward the horizon. The world opened by inches and then by yards. The sun found a seam in the clouds and stitched a thin, bright line along the edge of the day. James lifted his face into it and let himself, for a little while, be warmed.

CHAPTER 8
THE ILLUSION OF LIGHT

James had never camped before—at least, not like this. He'd gone on the occasional hunting trip into the forests near home, but that was nothing like the bare-bones wilderness camping he was doing now. The royal hunts had horses and porters and hot stew waiting in lidded iron pots; there were wool tents with carpets thrown down to keep out the damp and attendants who appeared out of nowhere to refill cups. Here, the world did not arrange itself around him. The ground was the floor. The sky was the roof. If he wanted warmth, he had to make it.

Lusin, on the other hand, looked perfectly at home in the wild. He moved through the stands of alder and willow as if he'd been born from their shadows, reading the lay of the land the way other people read a familiar letter. He chose a campsite that seemed, to James's untrained eye, like any other bald patch of earth—and yet it caught the last light, broke the wind, and sat just far enough from the stream to dodge its night chill. He knelt, touched the ground once as if greeting it, and the place felt—somehow—settled.

First, he led James to a clear stream to catch dinner. The water slid over rounded stones like silk over bone; it sang to itself in a bright, ceaseless whisper. Fishing was no new activity to James, but the method certainly was. Instead of rods or spears, Lusin simply waded into the current in his base garments—a fitted black crop top and leggings—and moved with uncanny grace. He was as at home in the water as the fish he plucked from it. His movements were smooth and deliberate, more like liquid than flesh. He didn't churn or splash; he simply… redirected the stream with his body, the way a reed divides a current without disturbing it.

When he reached, he didn't snatch so much as arrive with his clawed fingers where the trout already intended to be. James could only stand at the shore and stare (he called it observing), cheering under his breath whenever Lusin surfaced triumphantly with another catch, scales flashing silver in the shallows.

Lusin's skin beaded with water; droplets clung to the fine scales like dew on enamel. He pushed a strand of pale hair from his face with the back of his wrist and, with a mischievous gleam in his golden eyes, he eyed a large trout, lunged, and caught it in his mouth—its body neatly impaled on a pair of long, fine snake fangs.

James definitely did not find it adorable when Lusin turned to beam at him, squinty-eyed, the floppy fish hanging from his mouth like a prize. He also absolutely didn't notice how the droplets ran down his lithe frame, or how the long muscles of his back moved under skin like a cat's when it stretches, or how his heart skipped every time Lusin flashed one of those wide, genuine smiles that seemed to reach the parts of his face his patient smiles rarely did.

The light went from gold to pewter, and the air took on the blue edge evening wears when the heat leaves with the sun. Lusin dried himself and James volunteered to cook the fish, eager to feel useful—eager to have his hands occupied with something that wasn't fiddling with the hem of his cloak.

He gathered drifted twigs and a few deadfall branches, shaved tinder with his hunting knife, and built the fire the way Lady Anne had once taught him: small at first, respectful, coaxed rather than commanded. The spark took, breathed, and grew. Soon a steady column of heat rose, turning night insects into brief sparks as they wandered too near.

While he roasted their meal on green sticks cut from willow, the oils spitting and scenting the air with clean, mouth-filling richness, Lusin disappeared into the brush for a time.

The hush that followed his absence felt immediate. James listened to the low hiss of the stream and the soft percussion of drips falling from leaves, watched smoke write lazy lines against a deepening sky, and let the edges of the day unhook one at a time.

The fish crisped, skin blistering and cracking to reveal pearly flakes beneath. Fat hissed when it fell; the sound was oddly satisfying.

When Lusin returned, he was smiling again—less awkwardly now, as if his face was learning what it meant to be happy. Something small and bundled was tucked in his arms. He sat beside James, accepted a skewer of fish, and they ate in companionable silence, shoulder to shoulder, the sort of quiet that had weight without pressure. The heat from the fire and the residual heat from Lusin where he'd sat swayed and mingled between them.

Then came the crunch.

It was a delicate sound at first, like the first break of a hard sugar shell. James froze mid-bite and turned. Lusin had a clutch of bird eggs neatly wrapped in his sleeve, white and speckled, still warm enough to fog in the cooling air. One by one, he lifted them delicately to his lips, bit the top off with a crisp snap, drank the contents in a single clean pull, and discarded the shells into the fire, where they blackened, then whitened, then collapsed.

The sight was both grotesque and elegant, and James could not look away. There was nothing sloppy in it, nothing cruel; it was efficient and oddly reverent, like a ritual done properly without apology.

When Lusin caught him staring, he misread the expression and dutifully offered him one with his usual open generosity.

James refused as politely as possible, suppressing a gag that rose as much from the idea as from the texture his imagination insisted on providing. Lusin wasn't offended. He simply smiled and continued his meal, content as ever, as if James's preferences were simply more information to be stored alongside the weather and the direction of wind.

James returned to his fish but could no longer focus on eating for the way his attention kept circling back to the man beside him. Somehow, even this was endearing. The world had shifted its center and, inexplicably, cracked open something tender in him.

He decided to speak before his brain talked him out of it. The words felt like stepping from a warm tent into night, bracing and necessary.

"So… tell me about yourself."

Lusin tilted his head, looking genuinely puzzled. "Like what, James?" he asked, far too innocently for someone so dangerous. The way he said his name—careful, unhurried, as if tasting each letter—made James's stomach tilt like a boat meeting a wake.

"I dunno." James shrugged and pretended the shrug had always been the plan. "We're going to see your dad, right? Tell me about him."

Lusin's smile softened into something fond. It changed his whole face, softened the planes, made his eyes seem less like coins and more like amber.

"He is Radha, the Serpent King."

James choked.

The piece of fish lodged itself in his throat at the exact center of the worst possible swallow, and he flailed violently, making a humiliating assortment of sounds. The world narrowed to a hot point just below his larynx.

Lusin was on him in an instant, eyes wide with panic that didn't suit him at all. "James?! What's wrong?" His hands darted everywhere, searching for injury, making James gasp involuntarily—and the fish slipped deeper in the wrong direction.

Realization flashed across Lusin's face like lightning over water. He moved behind James in one fluid step, wrapped his arms around his chest, and squeezed hard, precise as a practiced strike. The obstruction popped free with an undignified wet sound, and James collapsed forward, palms braced in the dirt, gasping sweet oxygen before dissolving into a coughing fit that made his eyes water and his nose run and his pride shrivel.

Lusin patted his back anxiously in a staccato rhythm that might have been meant to soothe.

"Are you all right?"

James waved him off, face red from more than just asphyxiation. "R-Radha?" he wheezed when he could manage the shape of words. "He's your dad?!"

Lusin nodded proudly. "You know of him?"

Know of him? James almost laughed and did not, because he didn't trust laughter not to become coughing again.

Everyone knew of Radha—the most feared creature in all the lands. The master of curses and dark magic. The serpent lord who had trained Lord Xavier himself. Terrifying… and fascinating. The name lived in the back of every cautionary tale whispered to children; it lived in the front of every serious discussion about the boundaries of magic.

It was a name with gravity.

"You really think he'll see me?" James asked when he could speak without rasping.

"Of course," Lusin said simply. "He has wanted to meet my Sun for years now."

There it was again.

My Sun.

The phrase made James's heart flutter every time. He mumbled an uncertain, "I see," and focused on his food, which seemed suddenly to require concentration he didn't have.

Lusin returned to his eggs, perfectly content, as if they had just established the day of the week.

The quiet between them settled into something comfortable—the kind of silence that feels like the middle of a conversation rather than the end of one.

The fire burned down to a steady bed of coals. The stream kept speaking its single syllable over and over, insisting it meant more things if you listened long enough.

Eventually, James asked, because the question had been sitting lightly on his tongue for ten minutes, "You really like bird eggs, huh?"

Lusin smiled—wide and bright—and with it, the world brightened too, as if the fire had found a second source of light.

James smiled back before realizing he'd been staring again and decided to blame the heat.

They talked for hours about everything and nothing— the Wastes, the stars, their favorite foods, the color of dawn over the Great Sea. James described the way Solis's rooftops looked when the first bells rang and gulls lifted in slow spirals above the river; Lusin described heat that "cleaned you from the inside," and James leaned closer to the phrase like a plant to sun.

They picked constellations out of the thinning sky—when the clouds parted, there they were, patient and indifferent—and assigned them ridiculous names that would make any court astronomer faint.

James was surprised at how easily he could be himself with Lusin. Here, there were no titles, no tutors, no expectations. Just two young men under the open sky, their laughter crackling with the fire.

He'd never felt so free.

The night felt like a long-held breath finally released.

Lusin made him feel more accepted than he had ever felt in his life. The only other person he had ever felt close to feeling this comfortable with was Ben, and even then, James was still the crown prince and Ben was the noble tasked with looking after him.

He loved him dearly. He was his very best friend and he could even call him his confidant. But here, relaxing under the stars with Lusin, he realized for the first time how much that unspoken boundary between them had saddened him.

His mother had even offered him the opportunity to marry Ben and, if he were honest, if the time came where he were forced to choose a partner, Ben would be at the top of his list.

He felt a harsh stab of guilt about leaving Ben behind without so much as a goodbye, but he knew he wouldn't have done it any other way. He would apologize when he got home.

He slept—really slept—for the first time in days, and woke without the catch of panic in his throat.

James awoke to find Lusin watching him again, golden eyes soft in the early light—not the hawk's regard of a guard, but the calm attention of someone happy to discover the thing he'd been entrusted with had remained happily itself through the night.

The basilisk looked utterly awake, which made James wonder if he ever slept at all—and if not, where the weariness went.

The morning was the kind that smelled of dew, grass, and damp stone; the mist clung to their hair and then lost interest.

They continued their journey until they reached a small town stitched around a crossroads—whitewashed plaster, timber beams, a sagging inn sign that had once proudly displayed a painted goose and now looked more like a lopsided cloud.

Laundry hung like shy flags between windows. A dog slept in a patch of sun too small for its ambitions. Children sang in the morning light, the words of their rhyme only just audible:

four keys buried in the bones of the world.

James wanted to stock up on supplies—bread, salt, a half-wheel of hard cheese, maybe a packet of tea if he could find it—the type of simple luxuries that make the road kind.

He said as much and reached automatically for his coin purse.

Lusin hesitated, pulling his hood low over his face so that its shadow cut his cheekbones into sharper relief.

"What's wrong?" James asked. The question came out too quickly, more protective than curious.

"Nothing," Lusin said—too quickly, the way people say "nothing" when they mean precisely the opposite. "If you wish to buy supplies, we will."

"Then why the hood? It's not raining."

The words left James's mouth before his brain caught up and pinned them. He heard his mother's voice in his head— gentle, reproving—about diplomacy and gentleness and the way questions can be blades or bridges depending on how you hold them.

Lusin sighed quietly, not in annoyance but in the way of someone whose body has learned this breath by heart.

"If I cover my head, people assume I'm fae. It's easier that way."

Something in James's chest ached—small and mean and precise.

Lusin—who was radiant, gentle, extraordinary—had to hide who he was just to exist among people.

He couldn't stand that.

The thought of those scales, the very things that caught sunlight and made it into jewelry, being tucked away so that small minds could keep their courage—it made his hands itch.

He glanced around, then grabbed Lusin's arm and tugged him into a narrow alley that ran like a seam between a cooper's shop and a baker's storage room. Barrels sweet with the ghost of ale leaned against one wall. The cobble stone ground held a smear of chalk where children had been playing a hopping game and abandoned it mid-square.

Lusin allowed himself to be moved, though his expression was curious—head cocked in that birdlike way that revealed the fine pattern of scales adorning his cheekbone.

Once sure they were alone, James pulled back Lusin's hood.

The basilisk blinked, clearly confused, as sunlight touched the scales on his cheek. They shimmered like polished pearl, like the inside of a shell turned to the light in a fisher's palm.

James found himself staring again, wondering—just for a heartbeat—how they'd feel beneath his fingers.

He shook the thought away and muttered, "Hold still."

"James, wha—?"

He began chanting softly, hands hovering just above Lusin's face. The words shimmered on his tongue, threads of arcane magic weaving through the air. He felt the now-familiar tingle as the mark in his palm warmed—not painfully this time, just a reminder that magic cost something and he was choosing to spend.

A breath of pearly air stirred between his fingers and Lusin's skin, smelling faintly of crushed thyme and cold iron.

A brief flash of white light, and the scales vanished—replaced by smooth, pale skin.

"There," James said, wiping sweat from his brow with the back of his wrist and ignoring the quiver in his forearm. "That should do it."

Lusin touched his cheek, stunned. His fingers met skin where scales had been; his brows lifted, and for a heartbeat he looked very young—the way people do when they see themselves in a mirror and do not recognize what is returned.

"It's a simple illusion spell," James explained, grinning despite himself. "Took me forever to learn."

He hesitated, then laughed because the memory came whether he invited it or not.

"Actually, the first time I used it was… kind of stupid."

Lusin tilted his head. "What happened?"

"Well," James said, smirking at the memory that unspooled like a ribbon he couldn't resist tugging, "Ben and I were learning basic arcane illusions. The spell's hard—it burns through mana fast and only lasts an hour. But we decided to, uh… test it."

He could already hear Ben's horrified voice in his head, the long-suffering baked in.

So they cast the illusion on a dead rat to make it look like his father's crown.

Swapped it out right before a diplomatic meeting.

The spell wore off halfway through.

Lusin's eyes widened. "And?"

And suddenly the King of Valenor was wearing a dead rat on his head in front of three foreign ambassadors.

The image rose vivid as a painting: the glimmer of jewels becoming tacky gray fur, the slack little paws drooping over the King's brow, the collective inhale of a room trying to decide if this was a new custom or an omen.

James was grinning now, helpless against it. He could see his father's stillness—the way it went so very still it counted as a gesture; he could see one ambassador's mouth fold into itself like badly pleated fabric. He could hear—clear as if he stood there—the moment someone failed to swallow a scream and turned it into an unfortunate squeak.

Lusin blinked, then started to laugh—a clear, genuine sound that made James's chest tighten in a strange, happy ache. The laugh wasn't polite; it wasn't shaped to please anyone. It was delighted. It knocked against James's ribs like a hand wanting to be let in.

"I see why your teachers had trouble with you," he said between laughs.

"Yeah, Ben called it 'an international incident.' I call it art." James lifted one finger to wipe away a tear of mirth, still smiling, and decided not to dwell on the week of penance that had followed, or the way his father's exasperation had softened at the edges when he thought no one was looking.

Lusin was still smiling as James grabbed his wrist and pulled him out into the sunlight.

The street had warmed, the stones drying in irregular patches that looked like maps drawn by a child. When Lusin reached for his hood again, James batted his hand away and pointed to the dusty window of a nearby shop where a cracked pane held a wavering reflection.

"Look."

Lusin glanced, then gasped softly. He touched his reflection, fingertips tracing the smooth skin where his scales had been, then the line of his jaw, then the place beneath his left eye where the fine pattern had always caught the light.

The illusion held.

For anyone passing them by, he was simply an odd, beautiful stranger with too-pale skin and eyes too bright for the hour.

"It's only an illusion," James said. "It'll fade in about an hour—but you won't have to hide your face while we're here." He tried for a breezy tone and landed somewhere near earnest.

The truth was, the thought of Lusin shrinking himself to fit into a market stall's worth of courage made his throat tight.

Lusin turned back to him, eyes warm and impossibly soft—the kind of soft that wasn't weakness but trust.

"Thank you, James."

James blushed furiously, which his ears helpfully announced.

"You're welcome. Come on—supplies won't buy themselves."

He turned away quickly, partly to hide the color in his cheeks and partly because if he kept standing in that alley, he might do something disastrously honest.

As Lusin followed, James swore he heard him whisper— voice low and reverent, not to the air but to the shape the air took around James:

"Yes… *my Sun.*"

This time, James didn't bother pretending he hadn't heard it—or that his heart hadn't fluttered at the sound.

He let the word settle where it wanted to live and did not try to uproot it.

The market opened before them: stacked wheels of cheese with their rinds oiled to a dull shine; strings of onions like plaits of pale hair; bolts of rough linen spilling from a trader's arms like tame waterfalls; a child dragging a crooked-wheeled cart with a serious expression that belied the cart's rattling protest.

Merchants called prices in the singsong cadence of people who have made the same offer every day of their lives and still find a way to make it sound like a favor.

James bartered for bread that wore flour like snow, a paper-twisted packet of salt that crackled when he folded it, a wedge of cheese with the bite of grass still in it, and two small apples with bruises that promised sweetness.

The illusion would fade, the spell would run its course, the hour would fold back into itself.

But for now, in this small bright slice of morning, Lusin walked bare-faced through a town without flinching, and James—who had never liked markets unless he could race through them—found himself moving slowly, making reasons to linger, learning the shape of joy in the simple act of being seen.

CHAPTER 9
LUSIN VS SARAH

Traveling with Lusin was like living inside the happiest dream. The road unspooled in soft, sun-warmed miles; meals were simple and good; night after night James found sleep without bargaining for it. He was eager—desperate—to meet Radha and learn what he might know about the curse, but the longer he traveled beside the snake prince, the more he found himself wishing the journey would never end.

There was a steadiness to Lusin that made the world feel navigable. He watched the sky like a sailor reads water, chose paths that cut the wind, and somehow always knew where the ground would hold and where it would betray. James had never met anyone like Lusin—and he knew he never would again.

Days passed quickly as they made their way toward the Basilisk Wastes. The landscape shifted in slow, comprehensible gestures: green giving way to dun, soft loam to grittier soil, trees thinning until the spaces between them held more sky than leaf.

They skirted small towns where dogs slept in doorways and women swept stoops with twig brooms; they crossed creeks that babbled in quick syllables over stone; they cooked breakfast in fog and supper under a bowl of stars so crowding it felt like a festival. They spoke when there was something worth saying, and when there wasn't, Lusin's quiet was roomy enough to share.

Too soon, James found himself standing atop a long-backed hill overlooking the vast expanse of Lusin's homeland. It was dusk, and the massive dunes stretched endlessly into the darkening horizon, a sea paused mid–whitecap, all frozen wave and shadow. The last light gilded their crests. The air changed—dry as a book's edge, crisp as cracked clay. Wind came in long, clean lines that ran over the sand and pulled at clothes and at thought.

"We're almost there, James," Lusin said cheerfully.

James didn't trust himself to speak, so he only nodded. The motion felt mechanical, his throat too tight for anything broader. Lusin's smile faded, and he tilted his head with concern, the scales at his cheek catching the thin light.

"James? What's wrong?"

Those hypnotic golden eyes held his gaze, and James found himself mute despite the words clawing to be spoken: *These days have been the happiest of my life, and it's because of you. I should be thrilled that I'm closer to my goal, but I'm terrified that it means you'll leave me.* The words rose and broke without ever reaching shore.

"It's nothing," he said instead, forcing a weak smile that fooled no one. "I think I'm just tired."

Great job, James. Way to chase off the man of your dreams, he scolded himself silently, the kind of bitter humor he used when sincerity threatened to spill.

"Then we should make camp," Lusin offered kindly. "I'll take the first watch—you should rest early."

James nodded again, accepting the kindness because refusing it felt like a lie, though sleep never came. He tossed and turned, blankets twisting around his legs, haunted by the thought of Lusin disappearing into the desert forever— melting back into the place that had made him, leaving James to the echo of golden eyes and a word that kept lodging in his chest like a bright splinter. He knew it was selfish. The Wastes were Lusin's home, his destiny. Wanting more than he'd already been given was wrong.

A gentle hand brushed his shoulder, stilling his restlessness—a touch as careful as setting down glass.

"Rest, James. I'm here," came Lusin's soft voice.

Only then did James finally drift to sleep, not because the fear had gone but because the reassurance sat heavier than worry on the scale.

Dawn arrived uninvited, stealing away the fragile peace of the night with rosy fingers that pried at his eyelids. The world was colorless and clear, the air already beginning to lose what little softness night had lent it. James found himself stalling at every opportunity—dragging his feet, taking extra time to pack, double-knotting straps that did not require it, pretending to be fascinated by every passing plant and stone. He crouched to examine a stunted shrub as if it were rare; he squinted at a beetle's track like a map. Lusin noticed, of course, but said nothing, indulging his every delay with quiet patience that did not feel like resignation. He held space without comment, which somehow only made James more aware of every petty tactic.

Despite his efforts, they reached the edge of the Wastes by noon. The transition was abrupt: the light woodland gave way instantly to coarse, pale sand, as if a line had been drawn long ago and the world had agreed to honor it. Even the smell changed—leaf mold and bark giving way to mineral and sun. Lusin stopped and turned to him, the wind flattening his hair against his brow.

"Here, James. Eat this." He offered a handful of green herbs with small yellow flowers. "It's rue. It will counter the basilisk venom in the soil. You'll need to finish all of it to pass safely."

James chewed the bitter plant without complaint, jaw working, tongue trying and failing to convince his throat that this was food. He swallowed hard, eyes watering, and looked around, desperate for one last excuse to delay. That's when he spotted them—a patch of plump mushrooms basking in sunlight twenty feet away, caps fat and glossy as if oiled by the day.

"Hold on! If it's a long trip, we should grab those mushrooms. They'll help our food supply." He didn't wait for Lusin's response. With a nervous grin that tried to sell the idea to both of them, he trudged toward the patch, forcing his way through underbrush until he was crawling beneath a half-rotted log, dirt in his hair and his ass in the air. A twig drew a rude line up his calf; he bit back a yelp.

What am I doing? he wondered, feeling the heat build in his ears. I *don't even* like *mushrooms*. He reached anyway, because reaching was easier than walking forward. The log smelled of old rain and fungi and something coppery underneath, like a coin held too long. Before he could answer himself—before he could call this what it was, which was stalling—Lusin's sharp hiss split the air, carrying a warning that bypassed sense and landed straight in bone.

"Lusin? What's wrong?" he called, shoving backward, but got no reply—only the thunderous sound of trees exploding, a sound too large to belong to trees and yet undeniably wood-riven and final.

"Shit!" James swore. "Hold on, Lusin!"

He drew his hunting knife, wrapped it in wind magic until the blade sang against his fingers, and sliced through the dense vegetation before sprinting back onto the road. The peaceful trail was gone—transformed into a smoking battlefield.

Trees burned, splintered, and toppled; bark peeled back like skin; the air punched at his lungs with heat. Black smoke dimmed the sun and stung his eyes. Leaves turned to ash midair and blew apart like dirty snow.

Through the chaos, James caught sight of Lusin, fast and fluid, dodging fireball after fireball with the precise economy of someone who knows exactly how much space he occupies. James couldn't see the caster, but the fire bore the tight control and brutal efficiency of a trained battle mage. Flame licked over sand and died; where it found wood, it feasted. The smell of sap boiled to sweetness tangled with the bitter of char.

"James!" Lusin shouted, sprinting toward him—but the call left him open. A blast of fire mushroomed from the treeline and struck him squarely, the impact visible as a ripple through his body, sending him flying into a grove of burning trees. Branches broke his fall in a flurry of sparks and noise.

"LUSIN!" James screamed, voice raw as if he'd been shouting all afternoon. He threw the wind forward, the beginning of a spell already gathering in his palm, half-cast and hungry, when something yanked him backward by the scruff of his neck. The sudden force nearly snapped his spine; stars burst in the corners of his vision.

He kicked and thrashed, boots scraping dirt, heels finding no purchase. Whoever had him was impossibly strong. "Let go!" he shouted, voice cracking as he was dragged through the trees, shoulder bumping trunk, hip catching root. Branches whipped his face; his eyes watered and then refused to stop.

Finally, his captor slowed, and his boots hit solid ground, sliding a little in ash. James whirled, sword already in motion, slashing for the throat—only to hit air. His opponent ducked easily, a shadow parting around the blade, but the shift loosened their grip. James tore free and lunged for escape—only to be tackled again and pinned face-first into the dirt, breath shoved from him in a dull rush.

"Quit screaming, you idiot! It's *me!*" a familiar voice hissed in his ear, threaded with equal parts fury and relief.

"*Sarah?!*" He gasped, the word strangled and incredulous. "What the actual *fuck*?!"

"Is that any way to thank me for saving your life? Keep your voice down! He's going to find us!" she whisper-yelled, which was not whispering at all and yet somehow quieter than the panic demanded.

"What the hell are you doing here?!" James snapped, still struggling beneath her weight. Dirt filled his mouth with the taste of tin. He spat to the side.

"*Me?* What are you doing?!" she shot back, her own voice rising to match his irritation. "He's a basilisk! He was leading you to your death!"

"Who, Lusin? He wasn't leading me to my death!"

"I told you to shut up! If we're lucky, the flames will slow him down enough for us to escape—but only if you shut. Your. Mouth!"

As if summoned by the words—or perhaps because smoke and shouting are homing beacons—Lusin appeared behind her. His once white skin was marred by soot and blood, his clothes singed in ragged, curling petals, his golden eyes glowing faint red at the edges as if a coal lay banked behind each iris.

He looked furious.

Without hesitation, he grabbed James, yanking him free with a smooth, irresistible pull and shoving him behind his own body protectively. The move was quick and practiced and left no doubt where he would stand in a storm.

Sarah scrambled to her feet in a crackle of dry leaves, snatching up a fallen branch to shield her eyes—but it burst into flames at her touch, heat blooming up her arm like a greeting she had not intended to give. She dropped it and stumbled backward, eyes squeezed shut, her best attempt at protection against the threat of Lusin's stare. Then she hurled a fireball toward his face, heedless that James stood in the blast radius.

Lusin swatted the spell aside like it was nothing, a contemptuous flick that turned roaring heat into a guttering ribbon that vanished up into the canopy. The air rippled; the fire went where the wind wanted.

"You will not take James from me," he said, voice unnervingly calm. The calm of deep water. The kind that scares more than shouting.

Sarah fired again, a stronger blaze this time, hotter, faster, shaped with the bitter efficiency of long practice. Lusin countered with a cyclone of wind that lifted ash in a twisting column and blew the fire harmlessly into the burning forest, where it folded into what already was. Sparks drifted back like tired fireflies.

"James is my Sun," he continued evenly. "Anyone who dares to touch him will die."

James froze. Had he heard that right? The word struck him again with that same impossible mixture of terror and relief, and he could not tell if it made his knees weak or his spine straighten.

Before he could react, Lusin blurred forward and pinned Sarah to the ground. One moment they were ten feet apart; the next the earth itself seemed to buck and when it settled, Lusin had her shoulders in an iron grip, knees planting her hips. She kicked and thrashed, but his grip didn't budge. His claws gleamed in the firelight as he raised his hand, the point of each as clean as a needle, as unforgiving.

"Die," he hissed.

"Lusin—*NO!*"

James dove between them, the decision arriving in his body before his mind, pushing Lusin's chest back with one arm and holding Sarah away with his other forearm braced across her collarbones. The heat of Lusin's skin shocked him; the smell of scorched cloth sat thick in the back of his throat.

The basilisk blinked, startled by the interference, and in that instant the killing angle dissolved. He didn't resist.

"James…" Lusin started, the word both a warning and a plea, but stopped himself, jaw tightening.

"It's okay, Lusin. I know her," James said firmly, breath loud in his own ears.

Lusin nodded, though his suspicious gaze lingered on Sarah as if suspicion itself were a form of protection. She climbed to her feet, brushing off dirt in sharp, angry swipes and glaring at him with open disgust that was sharp enough to cut.

"Do you mind telling me why you're traveling with this… snake?" she snapped.

"Do you mind telling me what the hell you're doing here?" James shot back, heat finding a more familiar channel: exasperation.

"Isn't it obvious?" She rolled her eyes with a precision that implied long practice. "Your father—the King—sent me to bring you home."

"Well, I'm not going back! You can tell him I'll return when I've broken the curse."

"You're coming back even if I have to drag you!" she shouted, grabbing his wrist with the kind of certainty only people who've won many arguments carry.

Lusin stepped between them in an instant. His scaled hand clamped around her wrist; his fingers pressed into the tendons until she let go, an elegant demonstration of boundaries. The motion was protective, yes, but there was no gloating in it—only the direct application of "no."

"If James says he's not going back, then he's not going back," he said, voice cold but composed, the kind of cold that keeps ice from melting rather than freezes lakes.

James placed a hand on his shoulder to calm him, palm fitting the edge where muscle met scapula. "Thank you, Lusin."

Lusin relaxed under his touch, the tension easing as if someone had loosened a strap. He squinted at James as though looking into bright sunlight, then smiled—a small, helpless thing that lived briefly and completely.

Sarah's jaw dropped, her expression stumbling over surprise and landing on offense. "What… what is going on here? Are you in love with the snake?!"

Lusin's smile widened, amused, a private joke told by a face not built for deceit. James, however, turned crimson so fast he could feel heat radiate from his cheeks.

"What gave you that idea?!" he squeaked, betrayed by his voice. "And his name is not *snake*—it's Lusin!"

Sarah gawked at them both while Lusin quietly chuckled to himself, a sound that cracked soot into flakes in James's chest. James ignored his embarrassment, choosing instead to glare daggers at her, which was less effective than actual daggers but more sustainable.

"Fine," she muttered through clenched teeth. "Are you in love with *Lusin*, then?"

He ignored the question and turned back to Lusin because some questions do not deserve air. "Are you okay?"

"I'm fine, James."

A nasty cut on his cheek still bled, and his clothes were charred in places that suggested pain later, but the warmth in his voice made James's heart flutter, foolish and unrepentant. He had the sudden memory of the rue's bitterness still clinging to his tongue, and the impulse to fetch water, to clean the cut, to make useful replaced the urge to shout.

Sarah, meanwhile, looked ready to incinerate them both, fists balled, shoulders high, jaw set at that specific angle that meant *"I have not yet begun to argue."* The air around her had that hot shimmer that precedes an oven door opening.

James sighed and looked to the sky, which did not help because the sky was full of smoke. *She's never going to let this go*, he thought, resigned and weirdly fond, the way one is fond of storms that arrive when they must. He understood her— her duty, her love that arrived wearing chainmail and rules.

"Listen," he said at last, still refusing to meet her eyes because looking would make this harder. "I'm not going back. I'm going to see Lusin's father—he might know how to lift the curse. So you can march home and tell my father that."

"Like hell! I'm not going anywhere!" Her chin lifted. Sparks snapped from a nearby branch in agreement.

"Well, we're heading into the Wastes. Unless you've got some rue tucked away, I don't see that happening." He tried to sound practical rather than triumphant; the desert would make this choice for her if stubbornness didn't.

"I have some extra we can give her, James," Lusin said helpfully.

"L-L-Lusin!" James sputtered in dismay, whipping around. The desert wind caught his hair and turned his scolding into something ridiculous and, to his horror, affectionate.

Lusin blinked, genuinely puzzled. "But James, you said you know her—and you two seem very close. Shouldn't we allow her to come?" He said it like a theorem that balanced.

"She doesn't want to help! She just wants to drag me home!" The word "home" came out more complicated than he meant it to: longing and refusal braided together.

"I doubt she could surprise you like that," Lusin said fondly, the corners of his mouth tipping up, remembering a tavern, a room, a door, and a choice not to leave.

James's face flamed again. "Yeah… I guess you're right." It felt like admitting the sky was blue and somehow just as dangerous.

"That's not true!" Sarah shouted, breaking the tender moment with the precision of a hammer. "We both know you'd be out cold and halfway home by now if it weren't for your boy-toy!"

Lusin frowned in confusion—language turning into shapes he could not parse—but James exploded, full-body, like a spark hitting pitch.

"My *WHAT*?!"

The shout startled a flock of birds in a blackened tree; they tore up into the gray like bits of burned paper trying very hard to be alive. Heat rolled over them in a fresh gust from the fireline; ash sifted down, soft as dusting sugar and twice as unwelcome. For a heartbeat, no one spoke, the world holding its breath between the end of an insult and the beginning of whatever came next.

James realized his hands were fists, that his nails had marked half-moons in his palms. He exhaled through his nose, slow, felt the sting, and shook his fingers loose. He could feel the curse on his right hand thrumming faintly—as if offended on his behalf or merely glad to be noticed—and he tucked it behind his back without thinking, as if hiding it might keep it from being part of the fight.

Sarah's face had gone blotchy with anger and fear, the kind you only get when you care more than you intended to. Her braid was scorched at the end; she batted ash from her sleeve as if it were a thought she could rid herself of with motion. Lusin's attention moved between them, protective and bewildered, like a guardian set to watch two storms to see which would break first. He reached for James, then didn't, as if discovering that the bravest thing he could do was stand very near and not touch.

Wind pushed smoke down the road toward the Wastes. The dunes beyond the tree line waited, indifferent and patient, ancient as any argument about love and loyalty. Somewhere far behind them, a tree completed the long, terrible decision to fall and did, with a crack that sounded like a door slamming in an empty house.

Chapter 10
The Serpent King

James and Sarah walked the first few hours in stubborn silence. Their boots sank a finger's width into the hot crust wherever the sand drifted thick, then scuffed against baked flats where the wind had planed everything smooth. Lusin led the way placidly, unbothered by their drama, the swing of his stride unhurried, efficient, almost meditative. He seemed to read the land by feel—choosing lines of travel that looked arbitrary until James noticed how each step spared them a worse one: detouring a pocket of soft sink, angling across a slope so the sand did not avalanche underfoot, slipping between red rock outcrops where the heat reflected less fiercely.

As they traveled, the terrain grew less sandy, with red rocks appearing more frequently—tablets of rusted stone half-buried like old shields, then whole ridges lifted from the earth like the backs of sleeping beasts. The heat soared; the sun beat down relentlessly, a hand pressed to the nape of the world and never lifted. For the first time in his life, James envied Sarah's stupid hat. Shade-on-a-stick, he thought sourly, watching the brim throw a small, stubborn circle of darkness over her body.

He couldn't believe the desolation. There wasn't a skeleton of a single tree or even a rocky overhang to break the glare.

The air moved, but it did not cool—wind like a kiln's breath licking at ankles and wrists, sneaking under clothes to dry sweat into stiff salt maps. Every sound felt distant, thinned by heat: the scrape of leather, the soft hiss of sand, Sarah's rhythmic exhale. Even birds, if there were any, kept their opinions to themselves.

Eventually, he was too hot and exhausted to remember being angry with Sarah. Anger required energy and a sense of audience; he had neither. His tongue felt too big for his mouth. His thoughts—so quick and clever in the cool—stretched out, slow as poured honey. He struck up a conversation just to drown the silence and distract himself from the ache in his bones, from the steady drum of his heart in his ears.

"How did you find me, anyway?" he asked, summoning as much irritation as he could through the heat haze, though it arrived bleached and thin.

"Really, James?" she said, rolling her eyes beneath the hat. She wiped sweat from her brow with theatrical slowness, fingers leaving pale streaks in dust. "You aren't exactly low-profile. I asked around and showed your picture. Plenty of people had seen you and knew where you'd gone. It was so easy I could almost just use your name." Her mouth tilted smugly. "They also said you had a beautiful traveling companion who was white as the moon. Honestly, I started to assume you'd run away to be with a secret lover."

His mind flickered back to a lamplit room and a pair of golden eyes. He swallowed, throat rasping. "Stupid. You knew I wasn't interested in anyone," he muttered, managing indignation despite the heat and hating the way it sounded small.

"*Wasn't*, huh? Past tense?" She zeroed in on the word, as irritatingly observant as ever.

"You know what I mean," he grumbled, too tired to do more than blush. The heat made blushing feel like punishment; his cheeks prickled, then stung.

"Sure. I thought it was odd you managed to keep a secret like that from me." James glared, but it lacked voltage. "But the timing was suspicious enough to wonder. Imagine my shock when your 'lover' turned out to be a basilisk."

He winced. "Is that why you attacked Lusin?"

"Of course. I assumed he was leading you to your death. I'm still not entirely sure he's not." She flicked a suspicious look at Lusin's back. The basilisk paid her no mind. James envied him—envied that ability to let accusation slide off like blown sand.

"I trust Lusin," James said, and let the topic die. The words settled between his shoulder blades like a cool hand. His head pounded; the heat made talk feel like labor, and silence again became a mercy.

By the time the sun finally slipped toward the horizon, the color of the world gentled, though the stones kept their heat like banked coals. James collapsed messily against a broad red rock, sliding down until the stone caught him behind the ribs and stopped his fall. He squinted up at the sky and saw nothing but bleached blue and the long, thin lines of cirrus like scratches. Lusin hurried to his side, easing him upright with careful, unhurried hands, lifting as if James were something breakable. James was so tired his cheeks didn't even turn pink—enough to earn him an appraising look that felt more like a diagnosis than a judgment.

"We should stay here until you've rested, James," Lusin said softly. His voice carried the coolness of underground water.

James just nodded and let him fuss, too far gone to pretend he didn't like it. Lusin took the canteen, tipped it against James's lower lip with the same reverence he handled knives, and watched to make sure he swallowed. Sarah plopped into the sand and took a long pull from her own canteen. Judging from the lack of snide commentary, she was as wrung out as he was; even her hat seemed to sag.

James drank, savoring the lukewarm wetness and how it softened the tightness in his body. His muscles, clenched for hours against glare and grade, began to uncurl. The water tasted faintly of leather and metal and their own breath; it was delicious.

"How much farther, Lusin?" he asked, when air and words returned in partnership.

"Another day's journey, I'm afraid," Lusin said apologetically. Something in his expression suggested he wished he could make the desert shorter.

James flopped onto his back with a groan, the sound pulled from him like rope from a well. "I don't think I'll make it."

"You can make it, James. I will see to it," Lusin vowed.

That time, James did blush, but there was no heat in it—only a quick flare that left him oddly light. The promise wrapped around his ribs and held.

"Don't worry, Lusin," Sarah cut in, ruining the moment with the deftness of long practice. "He'll be fine. He's just being a drama queen."

James turned his head to glare but didn't move otherwise. Lusin gave Sarah a questioning look; James changed the subject before she could "educate" him into a worse opinion of himself.

"Good thing we've got plenty of dried food. There isn't even enough out here to build a decent fire."

Propped on his elbows, he finally looked. He'd been ignoring the view, focusing instead on the death march—boots, breath, the next patch of shade that never arrived. Now, it was almost pretty.

Golden-brown dunes stretched in every direction, their wind-cut curves repeating into comfort. Far to the east, the sand gave way to rock, and—faint on the horizon—the bright line of the sea, a silver thread pulled taut at the world's seam. Red stones punctuated the landscape, some cart-sized, some tower-tall, their faces pitted and flaked like old paint. Heat ripples lifted from them in visible waves, holding back the quickening chill of night the way a stove holds back winter in a kitchen.

As daylight faded, the dunes kindled with a poisonous, acid-green aura—the visible manifestation of basilisk venom. Ominous, yes, but oddly beautiful against the deepening twilight, like foxfire in a graveyard. The color sat just at the edge of seeable, making James blink and look again. Orange and yellow washed into ombré blues; stars pricked through one by one with a confidence a city's glow never allowed. The rising moon silvered the distant water into a fine, shining thread. The desert, which all day had shouted, now whispered.

"We should rest," Sarah said, interrupting the quiet. "If we start before dawn, we'll make real progress tomorrow."

Annoyingly, she was right. James had just enough strength to unroll his blanket, tug off his boots, and pass out beneath the stars. The ground was harder than any mattress and somehow kinder. He lay there and let the sky fall on him for a while. As darkness fell inside his mind, he was vaguely aware of Lusin sitting beside him, faithful at watch, the silhouette of him like a statue set to guard a tomb. It didn't feel like a tomb.

Despite rising before dawn, they found the morning had already been awake for hours, cool air quickly forfeiting its mercy. It was sunset when they finally reached their destination, because deserts play odd games with distance. Things that looked near took a day; things that looked far took two. The entrance to the Serpent King's caverns loomed like a gaping gray maw yawning in the desert, rock lips pulled back to show the long throat of the world. The wind that blew from it smelled of damp mineral and time.

As they drew closer, James blinked: for a heartbeat, he thought another Lusin stood among the jagged rocks—a mirage trimmed in steel. Not Lusin—but a man who could only be his older brother. Taller, hair cropped shorter and colored a pale, silvery gray instead of pastel blue. The same snow-white skin. The same golden eyes, stripped of Lusin's warmth. More scales too, covering most of his face and neck, their gray tone matching his hair so closely that at first glance he seemed carved. He wore black with silver accents—light armor, by the look of it—pieces fitted close for speed, not show. A long, thin scar crossed his right cheek like a deliberate brushstroke.

Lusin waved and hurried forward to embrace him. The elder's hard expression softened with fondness at the sight of his little brother; he returned the hug, though his gaze on James and Sarah remained cold enough to raise gooseflesh even in this heat. The look measured and found wanting, then reserved judgment for later.

"It's okay, Tehi," Lusin said, beaming up at him. "I've finally found my Sun."

The words were simple; the certainty in them was not. Tehi studied Lusin a long beat—eyes moving as if reading, as if the answer might be written in the way Lusin held his shoulders. Then he turned an unreadable look on James. Unease prickled down the prince's spine. The look was less than approving, to put it mildly. Hopefully Lusin's family wouldn't decide he wasn't worth speaking to and opt to eat them instead. Sarah would never let him live it down—in this life or the next. He imagined the headline: Prince Finds Love, Is Eaten. He did not smile.

"If that is so," Tehi said at last, "then we should see Father immediately. He will be pleased—and eager to speak with Prince James."

He lifted a scaled hand and gestured them onward. The gesture was spare, but it brooked no refusal. James startled at the sound of his name, then chided himself—of course they would know who he was. He obediently followed the two serpent princes; Sarah trailed reluctantly at a distance, hat brim low, resentment tucked under it. Cool, damp air embraced James's sun-scorched skin as they descended, every step like stepping into a deeper shade.

They entered a vast, winding network of caverns draped in flowing stone. The first passages were rough—walls like melted candles, water's handwriting everywhere. Left, right, center, right again—James gave up keeping track after the first turn. The spiraling tunnels knotted into a labyrinth that made his gut twitch at the thought of getting lost. Sound changed, too, becoming thicker, caught and thrown back by curves. Their footsteps echoed in a cadence that made the heart want to match it.

Moisture slicked the walls where minerals bled through in pale, delicate fronds. Here and there, low pools held water black and smooth as glass, reflecting torchlight as a scatter of coins. The air tasted faintly metallic—iron, stone, a whisper of something living that had never seen sky. James ran his fingers across a band of rock and came away chalky, the dust crisp on his skin.

Eventually, packed dirt gave way to cut stone underfoot. The slope smoothed into broad stairs, and they descended into the largest natural chamber James had ever seen. It swallowed sound whole and gave back a softened, solemn version. A green velvet carpet ran the length of what could only be a throne room, its nap crushed in a central line where feet had passed for years.

The air was warmer here, humid and scented like deep earth and old incense. Massive pillars—each carved with coiling serpents—rose into a ceiling drowned in darkness. The empty eyes of stone snakes watched as the four of them passed, their stone tongues frozen mid-flick.

On either side, alcoves housed artifacts James did not examine closely—bowls of hammered metal, lengths of embroidered cloth, masks whose eyes he did not wish to meet. The light was steady and strange, torches burning with flames that seemed to ripple slower than fire should. He did not look too hard at them either.

Ahead, steeped in shadow, a wide stone dais held an enormous green cushion large enough to serve as a bed for a small dragon. As they drew closer, something on it moved—a shift like a long exhale.

A long, rolling hiss filled the chamber. Weight—presence—poured through the space, suffocating and absolute, pressing against skin and mind. The black mass rose, towering. A gigantic serpent lifted itself to its full height, scales drinking light, twin yellow eyes burning in the dim like lanterns held deep in a void.

James wanted to run. His muscles refused him. He stood, nailed to the floor by the old animal part of his brain that remembered when such eyes meant the end of the story, while the beast regarded them—considered them, the way a storm considers a house.

"Lusssin," the Serpent King hissed, unmistakable glee in the sound, like a smile revealed in a darker room.

The creature slithered forward. As it came, its shape flowed and shrank, as if the idea of *serpent* were being folded smaller and smaller until, stepping into the torchlight, it was not a monster but an ageless and androgynous figure in silk: Radha, the Great Serpent King.

He was one of the strangest beings James had ever seen, and he had seen plenty enough strange lords and dignitaries to be fussy. Thick, ink-black hair fell almost to his ankles, gathered simply at his back; shoulder-length bangs framed a thin, bloodless face cut with such precision it might have been carved rather than grown.

His eyes were cruelly beautiful—almond-shaped, yellow, slit-pupiled—ringed in purple that bled toward the inner corners and traced the sides of a narrow nose like bruised kohl. His lips were colorless, his expression placid in the way of deep rivers. Unlike his sons, no scales showed in his human form; the smoothness of his skin made him seem more alien, not less.

A white silk robe, embroidered delicately with green serpents and edged in forest green with silver accents, draped his slender frame. It hung with the heavy fall of good silk. Simple—yet no one could mistake his royalty; the room itself behaved differently around him, the air tightening and then relaxing on his breath.

"Welcome home, my ssson," Radha said, his features warming at the sight of his youngest. The warmth looked odd there, like a candle in a temple of stone.

"Father," Lusin replied, his own face brightening. He stepped into Radha's embrace—an easy, unquestioning motion that made something in James unclench—then turned, gaze softening as it landed on James.

"This is my Sun, Prince James."

Radha's eyes widened slightly—that fractional widening somehow as dramatic as a gasp. He studied James with unblinking interest, head tilting the barest degree as if to catch a reflection from a different angle. The prince fought the urge to squirm, to tug at his clothes, to check whether the dust had made him ridiculous. Being looked at by Radha felt like being read.

"Well done, my child," Radha said, pride easing his voice so subtly James might have missed it if he had not been watching Lusin. Then, formally, "Welcome, Prinssse Jamesss. Long have I desssired to meet you. I thank you for returning my ssson to me in good health."

The politeness threw James for a beat. He had braced for menace or disdain or both; he had not prepared for court manners carried on a hiss. *Diplomacy,* he reminded himself.

He straightened and bowed, feeling the grit along his collar, the salt stiff in his sleeves.

"Lord Radha, Serpent King. Thank you for agreeing to see me. Our journey was long, but good."

"There isss no need for formalitiesss, young one," Radha said, amusement flickering in those hard eyes like light striking metal. "You have long been expected."

Was the old king teasing him? James couldn't quite tell. Radha's chuckle suggested yes, but the sound came from a mouth that had said far worse things softly. His skin pebble-pricked under his shirt.

"It seems there is something you wish to discusss with me," Radha prompted gently, as though coaxing a shy animal out of brush.

James blinked, remembering why he'd come, aside from escorting Lusin home. The latter thought sent a small, bitter sting through his heart; he ignored it, and the ignoring stung worse. He drew a breath that smelled of silk and stone.

"Yes, Your Majesty," he said out of habit.

Radha's eyelids lowered a fraction, tolerant.

"I've come to ask your counsel. Do you know anything about this curse"—he held out his palm—"and about the mage Sahir who cast it?"

The change in Radha was immediate and total. Whatever he'd expected, it wasn't that. His expression fell into severity the way a face falls into sleep—completely, without residue of what came before. He stepped closer, studying the mark with those unsettling eyes, his fingers hovering just above James's skin as if heat alone could tell him what he needed to know.

"Yesss," he said slowly. "I know of Sssahir." A pause, then: "I am familiar with his cursesss. Young one, regrettably, your sssituation is dire."

The rune in James's palm pulsed once, as if it recognized the Serpent King—and answered him.

The floor seemed to vanish beneath James. The word *dire* landed with a clean edge. He'd known it was bad. He hadn't imagined critical. It hadn't even felt entirely real until now. It had been a problem to solve, nothing more than an errand added to a list. He stared at nothing, wide-eyed, dimly aware of Sarah's gasp—sharp and unmasked—and the shocked fear shadowing Lusin's face as if a cloud had crossed a sun that did not know how to be dim.

"C-can nothing be done?" he managed. The question came from somewhere lower than his throat, somewhere that remembered being a child.

Radha weighed him with another long look, then lifted his gaze toward some middle distance, as if reading from a shelf only he could see. "I believe there may be sssomething," he said at last, "but it will be difficult. It would be best to ssspeak more over dinner. There are things I must consssult first. Tehi, show our guestsss to their accommodations. Lusssin, come with me."

With that, the Serpent King turned down a side corridor, silk whispering, hair trailing like ink poured along the floor. Tehi pivoted with soldierly economy, already angling toward a different passage that smelled of cool stone and clean water. Lusin shot James a longing look—bright and quick, a thrown rope—and for a beat it was just the two of them in a room full of snakes and kings. Then he hurried after his father, steps soundless, and James felt the absence like a hand removed from his shoulder.

He exhaled, not realizing until then that he had been holding his breath. The air he pulled in tasted of questions and old answers. Sarah adjusted her hat, the brim trembling slightly, and for once said nothing at all.

CHAPTER 11
TRUST

"I am sssorry, my child," Radha said to his favorite as he swept through the earthen corridors, Lusin trailing half a step behind. "After King Alfred'sss announcement, I asssumed Prince James had come to asssk for your hand. I wisssh I had known you were coming under far more dire circumstancesss."

His voice carried the soft scrape of silk along stone, a measured hush that made the torches seem to bow their flames inward. The corridor they moved through was long and steady, its floor smoothed by centuries of passing feet and coils; the walls shone with the faint wet of an underground breath, mineral-scents rising in cool waves that tempered the desert's heat. Torchlight stitched and unstitched shadows along the serpent-carved pillars at regular intervals, as if the rock itself were breathing with them.

Radha glanced back. Lusin's eyes were fixed on the floor ahead, focused on nothing; his face was set like stone, his brow dotted with tiny beads of sweat. He walked with all his usual grace, but his hands betrayed him—fingers opening and closing once, then steadying against his sides as though bracing against a tremor only he could feel. Radha slowed, letting him catch up, and set a comforting hand on his shoulder. The touch was light, almost ceremonial, but the pressure beneath it was real. Lusin refused to meet his gaze.

"Father… tell me. Can James be saved?" His voice was quiet, desperate—so unlike the even, curious tone he used for every other question that it seemed to drop the air around them two degrees.

"We have no choice. We mussst sssave him," Radha answered. The hiss held no indulgence, only a flat truth stated as law. "Every curssse, without exception, hasss a counter. We must find and perform it quickly. It would not do for you to have found your Sssun only to lossse him again so sssoon."

They continued in urgent silence, the kind that was not emptiness but concentration, until they reached Radha's personal library. The doors here were old wood banded with iron, not for strength but for memory, carved densely with the looping script of hands now long dust. Radha pressed them, and they opened with a sigh like a book's first page.

Fortuitously, he knew of Sahir and was familiar with his curses; that would make the research swifter. Still—*Sahir*. The name rasped against even Radha's practiced composure. He tucked the reaction where he stored weather and grief and stepped into his haven.

Radha had always been fond of this place—a haven heavy with the scent of aging parchment and memory. The room was massive, larger even than the throne room, but the scale did not intimidate; it invited. Light gathered here differently, warmer, as if the lamps had learned gentleness among paper and ink.

Rows of floor-to-ceiling wooden shelves sagged under thousands of leather-bound tomes. Most were not books, but his own journals: eons of history and personal recollection, spines creased by time and his own hands. Along the walls, small ladders waited in their rails, scuffed where he had climbed in other bodies to fetch the same knowledge.

He went to the oldest bookcase and scanned the spines, his fingers caressing aged leather until he found what he sought. The bindings were labeled in his narrow, precise hand: a single word, a date, sometimes only a sigil. Lusin watched his every move, outwardly patient, eyes glittering with anxiety in the torchlight the way a lake glitters when wind insists on it.

"Do you remember something that will help James?" Lusin asked as Radha freed several volumes. His voice surprised itself with its steadiness.

"I believe I do. I came here firssst to confirm detailsss." Cradling the precious works, he glided to a well-worn chair whose arms bore faint crescent impressions of his rings. Lusin followed and, ignoring the other seats, settled at his father's feet to wait. He folded himself there with the same economy of motion he used for everything, spine straight, hands open on his knees as if for blessing.

Radha read for hours, combing through centuries of memory. The scratch of pages, the soft tick of cooling lamp glass, the distant drip of cave-water—these became the measure of time. When he turned a page, dust motes lifted, eddied in lamplight, and fell again. He skimmed where he could, slowed where he must, his finger riding the lines like a blind man reading braille. His mouth moved now and then in silent recitation, old equations of pattern and counter-pattern reassembling behind his stern eyes.

Lusin waited—calm and detached on the surface, but Radha knew better. Beneath the stillness, impatience gnawed; anxiety for James was tearing him raw, and waiting was an act of will. Every few minutes, a small tell betrayed him: a breath held longer than necessary, then released in apology; a flinch at the scrape of a page; his heel pressing, releasing, as if the stone could be urged to give its answer faster.

He stared without seeing at the seam where two flagstones met, and in that seam imagined a thousand little futures. The sound of James saying his name. The feel of James's hand jerking under his when pain ran up his arm. The way the prince's smile landed on him like light.

Despite the crisis, Radha allowed himself a quiet satisfaction. His efforts to secure a guiding light for Lusin had succeeded. The boy had obtained Prince James—exactly as intended—and had fallen wholly in love with his Sun. Pride twisted Radha's thin lips into the barest smile. It was not a soft expression; even his pride wore armor. But it was pride.

He lifted another journal from the stack, this one older, the leather thin as skin. A pressed sprig fell out—some desert herb now extinct in the upper dunes. He set it aside with care and read on. His handwriting shifted across centuries like the same voice at different ages: youthful flourish condensing into the economical strokes of a sovereign. He tracked Sahir through these pages where the mage had crossed his long life as shadow crosses a wall—similar each time, different in posture.

"Father? Have you found the way to save James?" Lusin's composure cracked. The question came quicker than the ones before, hopping the gap between his thoughts and his mouth.

Radha blinked out of paternal reverie and back to the task. The solution was not yet in hand. He had uncovered the curse's true nature and a direction for the counter, but not the precise working or its elements. He closed the book and set his hand flat on its cover as if to stall impatience with pressure.

"Almosssst, my child," he said, soothing. He knew the shape of "almost" could be a cruelty if given without care; he weighted it with promise. Lusin nodded and fell silent again, but his shoulders eased a fraction, the line of his mouth losing its pinch.

Pity stirred in Radha—not the condescending kind, but the old-world pity that is half kin to rage. Lusin had only just found his Sun; to plunge him back into cold darkness would be unforgivable. They had come too far. Losing James would jeopardize everything—and might even cost Radha his favorite son.

Lusin was strong, but still young; his mind and heart were tender, for all their discipline. Such a loss could break him along a seam Radha knew too well. Radha would not allow it. He returned to his research in earnest, turning to a section of journals marked not by title but by the absence of one: the silent volumes he had left unnamed because names gave them too much dignity.

The children would face many obstacles, but together they could succeed—*if* he placed the right tools in their hands. With luck, he might yet feast at Lusin's wedding. The thought drifted across his mind not idly, but like a prayer uttered in a language he did not admit to speaking.

He read until the lamp nearest him guttered and another, unbidden, brightened to cover the lapse.

James and Sarah followed Tehi in silence through a maze of great caverns. Sound transformed itself here into something with edges—footsteps clicking into the dark and returning thinner, voices swallowed whole, the faint sibilance of air sliding past crystal ribs. They walked what felt like miles, the passages twisting between glossy rock walls. Sometimes the ceiling lowered, forcing even James to bow his head; sometimes it soared out of sight and their torch flames could not persuade the darkness to tell them how high. Cool breathed on the skin where heat had lived for days, and sweat dried to a clean salt.

James hated the quiet but could think of nothing that didn't sound stupid to say to Lusin's older brother, so he focused on the scenery—and found it easy to do so. Lusin's home was more spectacular than anything he had imagined. It was not the spectacle of palaces—gild and array—but the kind carved by water and time with a patience that made kings look rash.

Beauty and strangeness mingled until he felt like an intruder in a secret world of marvels and hush. Stone seemed to flow from ceiling to floor, stalactites and stalagmites reaching, failing, reaching again across eras, some finally kissing to form pillars veined with faint yellow and milk-white. Pools of water lay so clear and still their surfaces were nearly invisible, betrayed only when a dropped grain of sand dimpled them, rings expanding like the slowest of clocks.

They passed a vast chamber dusted with snowy crystals that would put diamonds to shame—each point catching the torchlight and throwing it in a scatter that made the air look full of faint stars. They crossed an ivory rock-crystal outcropping arcing over an underground river that slid like ink into the void, its surface black as pitch until the torchlight drew silver on it like calligraphy. James leaned over the edge and felt the cool lift and stroke his face—river-breath, old and mineral-sweet.

They entered a hall whose ceiling vanished in velvet black, where green stars hung suspended in darkness, betraying nothing of their mystery. James stared the longest here, in the mystical dark dotted with green fairy lights. The effect was both cathedral and forest at once, radiating a feel of *sacred* that no other place could dream to possess.

Before James tired of exploring with his eyes, they stopped in a narrow tunnel at a simple metal door set into the damp rock. A single torch burned in an iron bracket beside it, its flame steady in a way fire seldom was aboveground. James felt nothing foreboding about the door—nothing welcoming either. It was a statement door: we keep; we close; we open when we decide.

Tehi turned the handle. The door groaned open, voicing the small complaint of well-made things asked to work after rest. Within lay a respectable-sized room cloaked in shadows. They crossed the threshold and waited while Tehi lit the lamps—three of them, one to each corner and one on the low table. Warm light revealed a comfortable, if simple, space with all necessary comforts and none of the clutter that defined the palace rooms James knew.

On either side of the rectangular room stood matching full-sized beds dressed in green, each with dark carved head and footboards. The carving was not ornate but meticulous: a repeating braid pattern, a pair of mirrored serpents whose bodies became the rails. Carved nightstands flanked them, a porcelain pitcher and basin gleaming on each polished top, a folded stack of linen towels carefully squared. A single plush chair sat at the edge of a round green rug that matched the bedding and upholstery. The chair's arms showed the faint shine of oil from hands; someone sat here sometimes, even if not lately.

Natural rock walls gave the room the caves' cool, humid breath; despite its earthen nature, the room was clean and free of dust. Surprising, given the door's protest of disuse. A niche in the wall held a small shelf with lidded jars—herbs? salts?—and a lopsided little sculpture of some pale stone like a child's attempt at a snake, which made the room suddenly feel less ceremonial and more lived in. James did not know why that comforted him, but it did.

"This is your room. I'm sure you will find it comfortable," Tehi said, almost emotionless, startling James from his observations. Tehi was not rude, but his manner lacked the deference James had been taught was due a crown prince. Then again, Tehi was Lusin's elder brother—the serpent crown prince, presumably—and needn't be polite if he chose not to. He had his own crown to bear, and in his house he bowed to none. James, however, had every reason to make a good impression.

"Y-yes," he stammered, rallying. "This will do nicely. Thank you very much." His voice did that unfortunate thing where gratitude arrived with a stumble; he straightened his shoulders as if posture could edit the sound after the fact.

Tehi's unreadable look lingered a beat, then slid to Sarah, taking in hat, red travel tunic, the stubborn set of her mouth. If he judged, he kept the verdict to himself. "Do not wander the tunnels. As you saw, they are vast, and it is easy to lose one's way. I will return later to bring you to dinner."

He left without another word, a slice of cool air following him as the door sealed.

That could have gone worse, James thought, turning to choose a bed—when Sarah reminded him she existed.

"Well, this is another fine mess you've gotten us into," she grumbled, having clearly waited until Tehi was well out of earshot before launching her latest tirade. She yanked off her gloves with little snaps, flinging them onto the chair so they landed perfectly aligned, which only made her fury look more organized.

"I don't recall asking you to come," James shot back. "Besides, this isn't so bad. I'm sure you've stayed in worse recently." He gestured at the room with a flourish that would have read as princely had it not ended in a small wobble of the wrist.

"Oh, yes, James. The room is lovely," she said, heavy with sarcasm. "Aren't you the least bit concerned that we are now *prisoners* of the *Serpent King?!*"

"Sarah, we are not prisoners. You really need to learn to relax," he said, rolling his eyes, though his stomach did a small, stupid turn that he refused to name.

"JAMES!" she snapped, voice sharp enough to shake fine dust from the ceiling. "Look around you! We are trapped in a basilisk's lair waiting to be eaten!"

"That's not true. Lusin and his dad are going to help us!" James shouted back, anger rising to meet hers—less because he believed he could shout her into reason and more because anything softer would sound like pleading.

"Use your brain for once! If Lusin is going to help us, then where is he?!" Sarah hollered, composure gone. Her hat skewed when she threw her hands; she shoved it back down, as if the act might nail her arguments in place. "Father once warned me that the magic of the serpent people isn't flash! It is deliberate. Ritual. If they curse you, it is because they *mean* to!"

"I trust Lusin," James bellowed. "He would never hurt me!"

He meant it. The certainty did not feel like bravado; it felt like architecture—something that had stood for a long time and would continue to stand without requiring his belief to hold it up. Lusin had given him no reason to think otherwise—and no one, not even Sarah, would shake that certainty. She stared, speechless for once, rage collapsing into a wordless gape that showed her as startled by his vehemence as he was.

"FINE!" she spat, channeling the rest of her fury into that single word. She spun on her heel, stomped to the bed on the right, and flung her precious hat onto it. The hat landed upright, judgmental even at rest.

James took the remaining bed, lay down, and tried to ignore her muttering—"idiot," "stupid," "going to die." The words came in loops, fraying, then knitting themselves again. He rolled to face the wall, stone cool through the blankets, the green of the coverlet a calm field in his peripheral vision. She'd see. They had nothing to fear from Lusin or his family. They would help him. He couldn't explain how he knew; he just did—down to his core, in that quiet place where answers arrive before questions are formed.

He curled his back toward Sarah, trying harder to tune out her fidgeting and half-baked plans. He listened instead for the sounds beneath the room's hush: the faint percussive drip somewhere far down the corridor, the sigh of air changing direction, a whisper he told himself was the settling of an imagined building and not some long, scaled body crossing a distant threshold. He had more important problems than the remote possibility of being eaten alive in a massive, beautiful basilisk lair. He needed to decide how to ask Lusin to stay.

However he framed it, the logic was thin. Lusin had fulfilled his promise: he'd brought James to Radha, who had thanked him for returning his son. What right did James have to ask him to leave again? Every argument felt selfish and small, even when he dressed it in duty—that he might need a guide for the road ahead, that having Lusin near would be strategically advantageous. In the truth that he dreaded he knew that when he left this dangerous, beautiful place, it would be without Lusin.

His heart ached, but he was determined not to let that be the end. Perhaps Radha would allow him to write. Letters could be lifelines. It wasn't what he wanted, but it would be a start. Lusin was a prince, after all. There were forms for these things. With time, maybe James could even request to court him—formally. He pictured himself asking in the calmest voice he owned, hands steady, breath even, as if the answer wouldn't decide the weather inside him for years.

He imagined the words and they slipped away, came back, rearranged themselves and refused to look less like pleading. He tried other tacks—humor, detachment, a ridiculous fantasy in which he shrugged and said, "Stay if you like," as if Lusin's choice wouldn't matter either way. He made a face at that version of himself and let it go.

He flipped his pillow to the cool side, pressed his cheek into it, and watched the lamplight paint thin crescents on the ceiling. He thought of Lusin's hands—cool and careful when they'd held his cursed palm, the slightest tremor betraying worry; of Lusin laughing, new and surprised, like a bell struck for the first time; of Lusin saying his name as if it were a promise. Each thought steadied him and hurt him by turns.

His thoughts slowed, meandering. The room's stone breath, the steady, stubborn heartbeat of the underground river somewhere in the bones of the caverns, the now-quiet rustle from Sarah's bed as even her outrage found the limits of wakefulness—these made a lullaby of sorts. His eyelids grew heavy. He drifted off to the sound of Sarah's ceaseless muttering—soft now, almost affectionate in its persistence—and the imagined weight of a cool hand settling on his shoulder from a corridor away.

CHAPTER 12
THE HEART OF THE EARTH

A knock on the door tugged James from his light rest. For a moment he didn't know where he was; a glance at Sarah brought it all back. She stared at the door, black eyes wide with apprehension.

He rolled his eyes and made a show of rising to answer it.

The stone floor was cool beneath his soles; the cave air moved with a slow, wet hush that smelled faintly of damp dirt and lamp oil. Somewhere beyond the walls, water ticked in a patient rhythm, like a clock that belonged to the earth rather than to men.

"You idiot," she hissed, ironically doing a commendable impression of a basilisk herself.

She had no time for more. James twisted the knob and threw the metal door wide—then paused.

As expected, Prince Tehi stood in the corridor: tall, emotionless, with the same vague aura of disapproval. Now, though, he wore handsome green and gold formal attire in place of the black-and-silver armor.

Pristine. Regal. Every bit Lusin's older brother.

James suddenly wished he had something better to change into. His dust-caked and travel weary clothes felt like rags beside the serpent crown prince's finery. He became painfully aware of how long it had been since his last proper bath. Tehi seemed to think the same; his cold golden eyes scanned James head to toe. After an awkward beat—James gaping, Tehi judging—the elder basilisk spoke.

"Father is ready to see you now. Please, follow me."

Neither rude nor kind. Merely toneless.

James floundered, then tried to regain poise. He smoothed a palm down his tunic, which did nothing to improve it, and lifted his chin a hair.

"Yes—thank you very much. Please, lead the way," he said with a respectful bow.

Tehi watched him a breath longer, then turned into the corridor. James could swear he had just resisted rolling his golden eyes.

James started after him—then realized he was alone. He backed up a few steps. Sarah hadn't moved.

"Sarah, come on. You're being rude," he hissed.

She shot him an indignant look, jammed her hat onto her head, and muttered an angry, "Fine," before hurrying after.

James growled under his breath and caught up to Tehi. Sarah fell in beside him, holding her tongue—but not her glares. For someone terrified of being eaten alive by basilisks, she might have taken more care not to offend them. Luckily, Tehi either hadn't noticed or (more likely) didn't care.

He led them in silence through long corridors and more spectacular caverns until a wide hallway of white marble opened into a chamber like the throne room, but better lit and with fewer pillars. Natural crystals glittered on the ceiling. Stone serpents lined the walls. Their eyes were polished darker than their bodies, so that even unlit they seemed to watch.

In the exact center stood a long table set with white linen and silver, laden with food. Radha and Lusin were already seated; they rose to greet them.

James's heart leapt at the sight of Lusin.

He looked breathtaking in finery that matched his brother's and complemented his father's robes. The cut was simple and exact, the green deep as river-moss, the gold at the hems catching light like water. He wore that adorable, still-unpracticed smile as James and Sarah approached. It might have been James's imagination, but those golden eyes seemed to sparkle with happiness as they took in his appearance—humble clothing and all.

The sight unknotted something low in James's ribs that he hadn't realized he was bracing.

Even while preoccupied with staring at Lusin, James didn't miss Sarah's mouth falling open in amazement—undoubtedly at realizing this was a diplomatic dinner, not a prelude to being eaten, he thought smugly. Her hat, which had looked warlike everywhere else, looked faintly ridiculous against this calm ceremony.

"Welcome, Prince Jamess and Lady Sssarah. Thank you for joining usss," Radha said, voice warm despite his cool eyes.

"Thank you for having us, Your Majesty. We are honored," James replied, bowing. Beside him, Sarah did the same. Her bow was crisp, textbook-perfect; if fear still lived in her, she had stuffed it into posture.

"Come and sssit," Radha invited.

James nodded and took the seat beside Lusin, who sat to the King's left. Radha naturally took the head. Tehi sat at his father's right, confirming James's suspicion that he was crown prince. Sarah sat across from James and beside Tehi—no doubt so he couldn't ignore her easily.

The chairs were sturdy, carved with the same braided pattern he'd seen elsewhere, comfortable without being soft. Servants—austere, silent—appeared and disappeared like thoughts, refilling goblets with a pale wine that smelled clean and faintly floral.

Up close, the table was a lesson in restraint.

The linen had a barely-there sheen; the silver was polished but not ostentatious. Porcelain plates bore a thin band of green at their rims. Between the place settings, low bowls held unfamiliar fruits in jewel tones and small dishes of something that looked like softened salt but gave off a delicate herbal scent. Warm bread rested beneath a folded cloth; steam escaped when a servant lifted a corner, and James's stomach betrayed him with a quiet, grateful growl.

"Prince Jamesss, you will be glad to know I wasss able to find what I needed regarding your curssse," the Serpent King began, going straight to business.

"We're grateful for any information you can share," James said, trying to leash his eagerness. His voice came out steadier than he felt. He folded his hands around the stem of his goblet to keep from drumming nervous fingers against the linen.

"I will tell you all I know, but be warned—it isss a lengthy ssstory," Radha said. "You knew Sssahir as a simple hermit and powerful arcane mage, but thisss isss not so. The truth is, he isssn't even human. He is an Old One, like mysssself. The flesh he wears now isss not his own. For eonsss he has worn the ssstolen body of an unfortunate human, and every ssso often he must replace his hossst. The process isss long and difficult. It requiresss forgotten arcane magic to cassst a complicated cursse. Casting it isss extremely demanding; any missstep means certain death—for both mage and hossst."

He paused to sip what appeared to be wine, savoring it as his words sank in.

Even the small sounds of dinner—the slide of a knife through fruit, the faint clink of a spoon—seemed to hush themselves.

"I'm... Sahir's new host?" James asked, barely keeping his voice steady.

"Of that I am not sssure," Radha replied. "Sahir's hostsss can lassst hundreds of years; I doubt he needsss a new one yet. However, the mark on your palm isss unmistakably that of the resurrection curssse. Whatever the reason, the fact remainsss: the curse hasss been performed, and time isss a factor. The rune will feed on your magic, leeching it from your body to ssspread. The more you ussse magic, the faster it will ssspread. When it covers your body, the curssse will be complete. In that moment, 'Jamesss' will be purged, and the Old One bound to the curssse will take your place."

A distinct chill passed over the table.

Sarah covered her mouth. Lusin leaned closer and gripped James's wrist. James stared at the rune on his palm—so innocent in appearance, quietly consuming him from the inside out. The skin around the mark tingled, as if aware of being observed.

He had the sudden, childish urge to scrub it with salt and sand until it vanished—and the equally sudden, adult knowledge that such an act would do nothing at all.

"Fortunately for you, young princsse, every curssse can be countered," Radha said at last, after allowing the silence to do its work.

James looked at Radha, daring to hope.

"But it will be very difficult. Even gathering the esssentials will be a tessst. The elements required for the counter-curssse are four arcane crystalsss taken from the Heart of the Earth."

Radha paused again, enjoying the weight of his words as he took a bite of his food.

James's mind spun with the amount of new information being dropped on them. He had heard rumors of at least a little of it: legends from the dawn of time that no one took seriously. Despite his considerable lack of knowledge of arcane magic, even he had heard of arcane crystals.

They made the other elemental crystals look common by comparison. They came with whispered warnings—rarer than the mages who could wield them, unstable, dangerous, and only used by the foolish or the desperate. Even the best struggled to create them and often refused, considering them too risky to exist.

Radha licked his wicked teeth with a fluid forked tongue, relishing his meal. He lifted a green napkin and delicately dabbed at his smiling lips, then deigned to continue.

"Gaining entry to the Heart isss not easy. It isss a living, sssacred place sealed away for eonsss. Four keysss are required to break the ssseal."

"Why would the Heart of the Earth be locked away?" Sarah blurted, curiosity overwhelming caution.

Tehi's sharp golden eyes fixed her with a look of displeasure. Her shoulders shuddered slightly, but otherwise she ignored him. James was impressed by her bravery.

Radha looked unbothered. He did not look at her but lifted his wine goblet and swirled the wine, which looked disturbingly like blood in the hall's light.

"At the dawn of thisss realm, the Heart of the Earth wasss born. It isss less a 'place' than a god-like being—the ssseat of power for all arcane magic. If it were destroyed, arcane magic would ceassse to exist. Yet its esssence was too strong; it twisted and poisoned anything that drew too clossse. To protect the fledgling world, the Elementalsss sealed the Heart. Even together, they could not bind it completely. In desssperation, they forged the keysss—one for each element—locked the Heart, and hid the keysss. Then both were lossst to time."

He let his gaze sweep across the table, lingering on James.

"Even now, the Heart still beatsss within the earth. Sssome say the Heart is not jussst power, but Will itsssself."

A cold shiver crawled down James's spine.

Radha's gaze lingered, distant. "There are truthsss even I did not follow to their end." He gathered himself and addressed James directly.

"Even if you gather the keysss and retrieve the crystalsss, you will need a truly powerful arcane mage to perform the counter-curssse. If it goesss wrong in any way, both the mage and Prince James will die. You face a difficult tasssk, child. And of courssse, removing the seal risksss releasing the Heart upon the landsss again."

He fixed James with a steady, warning look.

The dire weight of Radha's tone made James's stomach twist.

James nodded and glanced at the mark—then opened his mouth to speak, but Lusin acted first.

The table shifted with the force of Lusin standing, and the squeal of his chair echoed in the hall. "Father, I will go with him," he said, tone firm and full of finality.

James's head snapped up.

Lusin looked only at his father, expression serious. His scaled hand still held James's wrist—tighter now. Heat traveled from that grip to James's chest, a throb he felt more than heard.

The world narrowed to the space between their chairs; even the long table seemed suddenly too small to contain the promise inside that single sentence.

"Absolutely not," Tehi barked as he also rose, startling everyone except the King.

With both hands on the table and a furious look marring his handsome features, he glared at Lusin. "It is too dangerous. I will not accept my little brother risking his life for a foolish half-breed." His voice was low and dangerous.

"I want to stay with James. This is my will, brother," Lusin said, tone calm as he turned defiant eyes on Tehi.

Tehi skewered James with a scathing look, then appealed to his father—looking for backup, "You know well, father, some forces should never be woken." The air around him crackled with a cold that had nothing to do with temperature. Sarah's eyes flicked between James and Lusin, quick as flint.

"I believe the choissse is Lussin's to make," Radha said with a small smile. "Jamesss, if you are willing, I believe Lusssin would make a valuable ally in your quessst."

Tehi sat with the dignity of a crown prince, though clearly unhappy at being overruled.

James could hardly believe his ears. His thoughts scattered like startled birds and then returned, one at a time, each carrying a piece of relief.

"Yes!" he blurted—too quickly, too bright. "I mean—if it is your will, Your Majesty, I would be honored to have Lusin accompany me."

Over-polite, maybe—but he wasn't giving the King any excuse to change his mind. Radha nodded approval. Tehi's expression soured further. A muscle worked once in his jaw and went still; he reached for his goblet with the controlled precision of a man choosing not to say something harsh.

"Then it isss sssettled. Lusssin will go with you."

Lusin's grin flickered toward James. James's heart fluttered; his spirits soared. He wasn't going to say goodbye after all.

He let out a breath he hadn't realized he was holding and felt his shoulders drop the smallest degree. He may be facing a truly monumental task, something far worse than he had ever imagined—but he would not be alone.

Sarah, across from him, rolled her eyes so hard he felt the movement like wind; but even she couldn't quite suppress the way her mouth twitched—somewhere between resignation and relief.

"Fortunately," Radha continued, drawing their attention, "the keysss are ssssealed in the four cornersss of Valenor. I do not have their exact locationsss, but I will provide a tool to help you find them. Even then, gathering them will be diffi-cult and dangerousss; careful preparation isss essential. Even the ssstrongest mages risk madnesss or ruin if they channel too deeply into the Heart."

He took another slow sip of wine.

"Therefore, I will help you prepare for your journey."

The words did not ring like ceremony; they landed with the settled weight of action.

As if at a signal James could not see, servants began to move with new purpose. Covered dishes were removed and others brought, plates refreshed, goblets topped. The room's temperature seemed to rise by a breath; even the green crystals overhead brightened, or perhaps James simply noticed them more now that a direction had been given.

James tried, for a few moments, to pay attention to the food—he was starving and the dishes were both strange and wonderful. Then his gaze drifted again to Lusin, and the food became background to a more urgent nourishment: the nearness of the basilisk prince.

Lusin ate with the same unstudied grace he did everything, as if he had learned a thousand lessons in restraint and was now, finally, comfortable enough to let them be muscle memory. When he lifted his goblet, light laid itself gently along the curve of his wrist. When he turned to listen to Radha, his hair shifted like water, and James wanted to touch it with a curiosity that felt almost scholarly in its intensity.

Across from him, Sarah picked at her plate more than she ate, but the lines at the corners of her eyes had softened. Tehi, for his part, performed the act of dinner with the exactitude of a man who would not let appetite argue with principle. Only Radha looked as if the table were both feast and forum, his attention resting where it was needed and not a place more.

As they ate, Radha spoke not of lore but of logistics—what could be prepared and gathered, what basic provisions the lair could offer that would travel well across differing terrains, what information could be copied quickly from his journals into a form James could carry without adding dangerous weight. He did not belabor the point; he said enough.

It was a relief to James that even here, where grand forces were named, the world still turned on ordinary preparations: boots that fit, a pack whose straps would not fail, a coil of rope that did not rot in damp.

When the last course had been cleared and the servants had withdrawn into the walls as if swallowed by stone, the room felt both larger and more intimate.

The candleflames steadied.

Radha rested his hands lightly on the table's edge, and for an instant James had the sense—absurd and certain—that he sat at the border between a past he did not yet understand and a future that would demand all of him.

He glanced at Lusin.

The basilisk met his look and held it. No words passed, but the message was plain: together.

James curled his fingers under the table and pressed the pad of his thumb to the edge of the rune on his palm—just enough to feel it, not enough to activate it. The slight sting sharpened him, like a pinch before a plunge. He drew a breath, slow and quiet, and let it out.

They had a path, however perilous.

They had help.

And—most precious of all—they would be together.

Chapter 13
The First Key

"Fine! You were right, James! Can we let it go now?" Sarah cried.

No—James was never going to let it go. She would be hearing about this for the rest of her life. Not only had Lusin's family *not* eaten them, but Radha had given them a map marking the approximate locations of the four keys and the entrance to the Heart of the Earth. He'd even provided a necklace with a crystal that was supposed to serve as a compass. Best of all, Lusin had chosen to stay with him. His heart felt so light, he could have started skipping.

They stepped out of the cool caverns into the pale light of dawn. Even this early, the desert was already hot. Heat came in quiet waves, rising from the sand like breath. James and Sarah waited a respectful distance away while Lusin said goodbye to his family. Radha, Tehi, and a white-haired man James hadn't met stood nearby. Tehi still looked unhappy, but at least he wasn't arguing anymore. Radha's stillness held the gravity of stone; even at a distance, it steadied the air.

While they waited, James decided to study their new map. He crouched on a flat rock and worked the ribbon loose, careful with the parchment as if it might bruise. Sarah leaned over his shoulder as he carefully unrolled it. The map breathed when it opened, a soft release of scent—ink, dust, the faintest trace of bitter herb. It was richly detailed, a masterpiece of artistry and geography—mountains rendered in layered wash, rivers like threads of silver, the margins annotated with tiny, elegant hands. But it was the differences from his royal maps that drew his attention.

He recognized the capital and the Goldhorn Forest, the plains, the great Estredan Mountains, and the desert coasts. Familiar shapes soothed him for a heartbeat, then curiosity pried him forward. Four new marks caught his eye: one in the Range of Fire to the north, one deep in the Estredan Mountains, another buried in the Delta Swamps of the southern coast, and one here, in the Basilisk Wastes.

Each was indicated not by a gaudy symbol but by a modest sigil—four strokes that suggested a key's wards rather than the key itself. At the map's center, deep in the heart of the ancient Sylinthrae forest, was a rocky ridge labeled *The Heart of the Earth* in ornate calligraphy. The letters seemed to sit heavier than the rest, as if the parchment relented more under their ink.

"Looks like one key isn't far from here," Sarah said, tracing a finger near the mark in the desert. Her nail hovered rather than touched; even she respected Radha's generous gift.

"That's lucky," James replied, feeling optimism return. The word *lucky* felt almost profane in the shadow of what they had learned, but he kept it anyway.

"It's about a day's walk," she continued, ignoring him, "but finding the exact spot might be tricky."

"That's why we have this." James held up the necklace. The oval crystal shimmered faintly in the sunlight, the pewter filigree around it glinting like starlight. The chain was cool against his skin; when he shifted, the pendant tapped his sternum with a small, rhythmic weight. Radha had said it would glow brighter as they drew near each key, then dim once the seal was broken. James wasn't sure exactly what that meant but he was confident that they'd figure it out when the time came.

Sarah raised a skeptical eyebrow but said nothing. By then, Lusin had finished his goodbyes and was hurrying to join them. He moved like water rejoining a river; everything in James wanted to lean toward him. It was time to begin.

The desert burned in daylight and remembered it at night. For three brutal days, they traded one punishment for another: the glare's relentless hammering and the cold's thin bite. Sand got into everything—boots, blanket rolls, the hinge of James's jaw. It whispered when the wind coaxed it and roared when the gusts decided to peel the surface off in sheets. Their canteens grew lighter; conversation did too.

They kept the sea to their left like a promise. Some hours, it looked near enough to touch—a bright strip of turquoise the sun could not decide to bless or blind. Other hours, heat made it shiver away, and James had to force himself not to run toward a waterline that retreated with every step. He learned to ration glances as strictly as sips.

They made their marks on the morning with quiet rituals: Lusin checked the leather straps and supplies with smooth, economical motions; Sarah adjusted her hat, setting the angle as if that might tilt the day in her favor; James adjusted the crystal so it lay flat, then tapped the facets twice for luck. By noon, the rituals became bargaining—another hundred steps, another fifty, another twenty, then he could rest his shoulder against the pack's bite for ten breaths.

On the first day, the crystal stayed dull as ice. On the second, it picked up a whisper of light at sunset—maybe wishful thinking. On the third, even wishful thinking had sand in its teeth.

"James… maybe we should stop…" Sarah gasped. Her voice came thin, torn off by the heat before it reached the ground.

He wanted to argue, but his voice came out as a wheeze. "Okay. Let's head to the shore and rethink things."

The beach wasn't far, but every step through the burning sand felt like dragging his father's expectations behind him. He imagined himself as he had been at the palace—bright, polished, scheduled—and compared it to this version of himself, sweaty and stubborn with a map under one arm. For the first time, even adventure tasted like punishment.

When they finally reached the coast, James and Sarah fell heavily into the sand while Lusin lowered himself gracefully beside them, seemingly untouched by exhaustion. The contrast was almost obscene. James could not decide whether to laugh, weep, or crawl into Lusin's shadow and stay there until the earth fixed itself.

He couldn't help staring. Even travel-worn, Lusin's beauty looked effortless—his pastel hair gleaming, his movements smooth as water. The sight filled James with a mix of envy and admiration that made his chest ache. He told himself it was only because the basilisk was built for harsh lands; he knew it was not only that.

The air smelled of salt and heat. The water glittered every possible shade of blue under the high sun, its rhythmic crash soothing. The sound sanded his thoughts into rounds; he found himself breathing with the waves, in spite of himself. James was hot, filthy, and longed for relief. Without hesitation, he unbuckled his boots and peeled off his shirt. Cloth came away from his skin with a faint tear; the breeze kissed the damp beneath and made him shiver.

"You're not planning on swimming, are you?" Sarah asked, sounding scandalized. She had removed her hat at last and was fanning herself with it like a dignitary offended by the weather.

"Gotta get clean somehow," James said simply. He stripped down to his leggings and the crystal necklace and waded into the surf.

The ocean embraced him with delicious coolness. Salt tingled on his skin as sweat and grime slipped away. He let himself sink until the waves lapped his collarbones and felt his heartbeat slow. He ducked his head beneath the surface, savoring the muffled silence, then emerged with a satisfied sigh. Sound returned, softened—sea and breeze and his own breath. When he pushed his hair back, he caught Lusin's gaze fixed firmly on him. Those golden eyes didn't waver.

James grinned slyly. *Looks like he's not the only one who can turn heads*, he thought smugly. He tilted his chin just a fraction, and water ran in bright lines down his throat, knowing that even his pettiness had sunlight on it. Lusin's eyes followed the drops and his throat flexed with a subconscious swallow. James beamed.

"Lusin! Come join me!" he called.

The basilisk didn't hesitate. He rose then glided forward, shedding his outer layers as he went. His entry into the water was seamless—not a splash, smoothly joining the gentle waves. The sunlight crowned his pale blue hair in silver and made the faint scales along his cheek and neck shimmer like jewels. The air between them seemed to hum as James stared.

Lusin tilted his head, eyes soft. "James? Is something wrong?"

"No," James breathed, "everything's perfect—"

"If you two are finished flirting, how about catching us some fish for dinner?" Sarah shouted from the beach, her tone sharp enough to cut glass.

The spell broke instantly. James shot her a murderous glare, but she only smirked, triumphant. Lusin blinked between them, clearly confused. James sighed, defeated.

"Would you mind, Lusin? You're better at fishing than I am," he said sheepishly.

"Yes, my Sun," Lusin replied with his unpracticed smile before sliding beneath the waves.

James watched him go, the water gleaming where he vanished. He stood in the surf a moment longer, letting the cool gnaw at the heat knotted along his spine. Then he forced himself to scrub at the remaining dirt on his arms. When satisfied, he retrieved his clothes and washed them. He found a smooth, flat rock warmed by the day and spread his tunic there, weighting the corners with shells. Mundane tasks steadied him; their small successes were under his control.

On the beach, Sarah had given up indignation for efficiency. She sorted through their packs with the brisk competence of a quartermaster: tinder, flint, oilcloth, a length of cord she coiled and set aside. She looked up once, caught James's eye, and rolled her own so extravagantly he nearly laughed despite himself.

By the time Lusin returned—arms full of glistening fish—the sun was low on the horizon. Water beaded on his lashes and hung there like morning dew on grass. James cheered; Sarah tried not to look pleased and failed enough to be obvious.

It took little convincing for her to light a cooking fire. With a flick of her fingers a fire roared to life, and soon the smell of roasting fish filled the air. The flame burned a strange green against evening—her fire always did—and the color painted their hands and mouths as they ate. Oil crackled, skin crisped, and the first bite made James's whole body remember gratitude. They ate quietly as the night deepened, pausing only to blow on fingers and trade skewers for the better bit.

After, the world narrowed to bearable sizes: a circle of firelight, the breadth of a blanket, the measure of a breath. Wind lifted their hair; the sea kept time. The necklace lay warm where it rested against James's chest. He covered it with his palm. No light yet, only the pebble-weight of promise.

James stretched out on the sand, gazing up at the jeweled sky. The surf whispered, the green fire flickered, and the salt clung faintly to his skin. Stars revealed themselves with the shyness of first-night guests; then, realizing the welcome was sincere, they multiplied until the sky seemed crowded with old friends.

Beside him, Lusin sat as still as stone, eyes reflecting the stars. On the other side of the fire, Sarah scribbled notes into a small journal—the map reproduced in miniature, distances guessed at, water marks guessed again. The steady scratching of her quill had become almost comforting, a domestic sound in a place that resisted domestication.

When she finally stood, the firelight flashed across her dark eyes. "We should rest," she announced.

James nodded sleepily. He rolled out his blanket and settled in, the warmth of the fire fading as fatigue took over. He shifted once, twice, finding the right hollow in the sand for his hip. Lusin remained seated beside him, as always—silent, watchful. James's last thought before sleep was that perhaps basilisks didn't need to dream. Or perhaps, he corrected himself as sleep took him, they dreamed with their eyes open.

A chill woke him hours later. The fire was dying, painting the sand in pale green embers. The night had pulled its chill over everything. He stirred, realizing that he'd unconsciously curled around something warm—Lusin, sitting exactly where he'd been. The basilisk's presence read like a hearth without flame. James mumbled something incoherent, felt the blanket pulled more snugly around him, and drifted back into a deeper, safer sleep. Just before he dropped off, he thought he dreamed of a small star brought to earth, held in slender white fingers.

When dawn broke, cool and gray, the warmth beside him was gone. The first band of light made the sea look pewter; waves wore white collars. The wind had turned and came now from inland, dry and faintly metallic, as if it had touched rock older than names.

"Lusin?" James called, pushing himself upright. Sand fell from his hair and collar like spilled sugar.

He spotted him about fifty feet away, standing still and alert, facing inland. Something about his posture made James's heart skip. Lusin's weight sat differently over his feet; the easy openness of his shoulders was gone, replaced with a warning tension. James hurried to join him.

"What is it?"

"James, you need to see this." Lusin's voice was low, almost reverent.

He pointed westward. On the horizon, something enormous moved—distant, indistinct, but undeniably alive. It did not trundle like a caravan or sway like a line of palms in wind; it pushed its own rhythm across the land, too steady to be a storm, too whole to be flock. The light made a mirage of it, stretching its edges, tucking its center in and out of view. James had the unsettling sense that the land itself had decided to rise and walk.

Then Lusin opened his other hand. Between his pale fingers, the crystal compass was glowing. At first it was faint, like a flicker of candlelight. Then it brightened, pulsing with a rhythm—steady, alive, like a heartbeat.

Radha's gift was awake.

CHAPTER 14
THE KEY GUARDIAN

James squinted into the shimmering horizon, trying to make sense of the movement there. The dust clouds were growing larger, coiling upward into the sky like an approaching sand storm. Whatever was causing them was enormous—and heading straight for them. Heat bent the distance into a wavering sheet, the shapes inside folding and unfolding as if the desert itself were breathing. The Wastes often played tricks on the eyes, but this movement had weight. Purpose.

"James, we must prepare for battle."

Lusin's warning sent electricity spiking through James's core. The basilisk's tone was even—but sharpened, braced at the edges. This wasn't routine danger. This was something older than fear and louder than instinct.

"Sarah…" James warned, taking a half step back. The sand clouds rolled toward them faster than seemed possible. *Fuck,* he swore silently. Whatever it was, it was fast. The ground began to hum under his boots, a faint tremor that climbed into his calves and made the bones there feel hollow.

"Sarah!" He tripped in the sand as he sprinted back toward camp. Out of the corner of his eye, he saw her already on her feet, face tight with focus. "Get ready—we've got incoming!"

he shouted, fingers closing around the familiar worn leather hilts of his knife and sword. He yanked them free—messy but fast—and scrambled upright. The leather squeaked against his sweaty palms; grit bit into his fingers where the wrap had loosened.

His teachers would have berated him for such sloppy draws, but now wasn't the time for etiquette. He sprinted back to Lusin's side. The basilisk stood poised and still, golden eyes locked on the growing storm. James steadied his breath, channeling wind magic into both weapons until they thrummed faintly under his palms. The pulse of his magic traveled up his forearms like a low current and found rhythm with his breathing—*inhale, hold, release.*

"Any idea what's coming, Lusin?" James asked. His words felt small against the size of the dust.

Lusin nodded, his face grim. "I do. Be ready, James. This will not be an easy battle."

"So *what* is it?" Sarah demanded as she joined them, taking up position on Lusin's left. Her black eyes glowed crimson and lazy tongues of flame licked her forearms. Heat shivered the air around her, wavering the horizon into a painted thing.

"I believe it is… a basilisk," Lusin said evenly.

James blinked at him, disbelief momentarily overriding fear.

"If it's a basilisk, can't you talk to it or something?" he asked, half-hoping, ignoring how strange the request sounded even to him.

Lusin shook his head once. "This one has lost its mind," he said quietly. "There will be no reasoning with it."

Lost. The word scraped something inside him raw.

"We need cover—and don't look at it, no matter what," Sarah barked, mostly for James's benefit. She'd already angled herself so dune, wind, and fire all served her at once.

The ground trembled harder. Sand spilled from the crests of dunes in thin avalanches. The tremors became a continuous shaking—an approaching heartbeat, a countdown with no mercy.

James scanned wildly for something—*anything*—they could use as cover, but the Wastes offered only curves and exposure. The dunes were too soft and too shifting to rely on. They crouched low—Lusin beside him, Sarah a dune over—acutely aware that hiding here was like hiding behind a curtain in a bonfire.

The tremors intensified until James could barely stay on his knees. His teeth clicked; the taste of iron slipped across his tongue where he'd bitten the inside of his cheek.

Then the earth split with a thunderous crack.

Sand and stones exploded into the air, pelting James's face and filling his ears, mouth, and nose. He coughed, blinded, just as a guttural, sucking noise filled the world—then a shriek so piercing it ripped straight through his skull. He dropped his weapons and clutched his ears. The sound was more than sound; it was pressure made violent, a blade of air forced through bone and thought.

The stench hit next—decay and venom carried on a blast of hot wind.

Instinct betrayed him—he blinked grit from his eyes. He looked.

And immediately wished he hadn't.

What met his gaze was pure nightmare. The serpent rivaled the Serpent King in size, but where Radha had been majestic, this one was horror incarnate—its scales warped, crusty, and blackened, its back bent at grotesque angles. Pustules and tumors festered across its lizard-like head and narrow spine; one eye was sealed completely beneath swollen, decayed flesh. The beast was half-blind, half-rotted, and wholly mad. Its movements had the awful energy of pain: too fast, too jerky, too fueled by something broken.

Its remaining yellow eye bulged and rolled wildly as it screamed. Thick black venom spilled from its fangs, hissing where it hit sand.

James couldn't move. Horror pinned him. He watched the nightmare thrash. The air around it felt wrong—sharp at the edges, sour in his lungs.

"James!"

Lusin's voice cut through the paralysis—then impact. Something slammed into his side, throwing him clear just before the basilisk's tail obliterated the dune behind him. Sand blasted upward in a geyser. The shockwave ripped the air apart.

Dazed, he rolled to a stop and spat out sand. Sarah's voice reached him, sharp and furious.

"We have to blind it!"

"Right!" he shouted back, scrambling to his feet.

His weapons lay nearby, half-buried. He lunged for them, fingers closing around the hilt of his sword. Wind magic rejoined him with a crackle—eager, reckless, ready to spill.

To his left, Sarah hurled fireballs that burst against the creature's neck. To his right, Lusin moved like liquid light, daggers flashing silver as he struck for the remaining eye. Her flames illuminated the beast's wounds; his blades exploited the openings. The serpent coiled between them, a wall of flesh and shadow. Its body hissed where fire met rot; the smell was worse than death.

James leapt, driving both blades into its scarred flank. Rotten scales cracked, then gave way with a sickening, wet tear.

Putrid black blood sprayed across his face.

It burned like acid.

He gagged, stumbling back. His vision swam as the smell of death filled his lungs. The slime ate tiny paths into the leather at his wrist; the sting there would come later—if there *was* a later.

The basilisk screamed and whirled. Its tail slammed into his chest, hurling him backward across the sand. He hit hard near the beach, air bursting from his lungs. The world snapped to a single white point, then widened again with pain.

He looked up. Lusin was already striking again—daggers flashing, precise as lightning. Black blood poured from the beast's eye socket. Sarah flanked, fire chasing its movements, each spell timed to knock it off balance.

James forced himself up. He had no breath, no grace—only determination. He stepped forward—

And felt the crystal at his hip jolt.

The *green elemental crystal.*

The wind inside it pulsed violently—alive, insistent. Calling.

He fumbled it into his palm.

He had never actually used one before. Sahir had given it to him with the basilisk scales—an odd courtesy that he hadn't questioned much at the time. He'd all but forgotten about it. Now, it could be their chance.

He raised it.

It thrummed.

Wind coiled around his wrist.

The basilisk reared back, preparing to strike.

James tightened his grip until the facets bit into his skin.

"Please," he whispered.

The crystal *answered.*

A surge of emerald light burst outward—pure, clean, condensed wind given form. A shockwave blasted across the dunes, throwing sand high into the air. The mad basilisk reeled—staggering, truly staggered—for the first time.

Sarah gasped.

Lusin's eyes widened.

It was working.

And then—

The curse woke.

Pain shot up his arm. The mark on his palm flared white-hot—then darker, deeper, hungry. The crystal in his hand jerked as if something were pulling from inside it.

"No—no, no, no—" he hissed.

The light stuttered.

Flickered.

Collapsed inward.

The wind he'd unleashed didn't disperse—it *inverted,* drawn back through the crystal toward the spreading mark on his skin.

The elemental crystal cracked—hairline fractures spider-webbing across its surface.

Then it *shattered* into dust.

The power ripped through him like a hook dragged behind bone. His knees buckled. His breath vanished. The world tilted violently.

The guardian, though staggered, was still alive—and now enraged.

It lunged.

Lusin blurred forward and shoved James aside just as the serpent's jaws snapped shut. Its fangs found Lusin's hip.

"LUSIN!" James screamed. His voice tore raw.

He lunged—driving his hunting knife into the ruined eye socket. The basilisk howled, thrashing violently. Lusin's body slid from its jaws with a sickening sound that would stain James's nightmares forever.

Black ichor rained as the beast spasmed.

James dropped beside Lusin. The wound wasn't deep, but the veins around it were already darkening.

Venom.

Still—Lusin rose. Poisoned, shaking—but he rose. He stepped in front of James again, set his feet, and faced the monster.

James stared—helpless, useless.

Sarah was limping.

James's right arm was nearly dead.

Lusin was fading by the breath.

They were losing.

Rage boiled inside James—raw, electric. All his fear, his guilt, his weakness ignited. It rose like a wind desperate to howl.

He lifted his numb arm.

The curse mark flared—searing white.

"Stop—James!" Sarah shouted.

But it was too late.

The light erupted.

A shockwave shattered the world.

Sand and blood and screams vanished into blinding white. The impact pressed him open from the inside. A high, thin ringing filled his head—then nothing.

When the light died, the basilisk lay broken and still, black blood soaking the dunes.

James collapsed.

"James!"

Lusin's voice sounded distant—waterlogged. Someone grabbed his shoulders. His vision slowly steadied. Lusin's pale face swam into view, streaked with sand, poisoned veins creeping dark and terrible up his side.

"Lusin?" he rasped.

Relief flashed in golden eyes. Lusin's hands moved over him—checking for wounds, urgent, trembling.

"I'm okay," James whispered—though it hurt to lie.

Sarah limped closer, bruised and shaking.

Then James lifted his right hand.

The gasp they shared was sharp enough to cut the air.

The rune pulsed darkly beneath grime—its single mark now branching outward like black vines. Two leaf-shaped sigils unfurled below it, curling toward his wrist, while twin arcs looped around the edges of his palm.

He turned the hand over.

A circle and crescent gleamed faintly on the back of it.

The curse was spreading.

CHAPTER 15
ESCAPE FROM THE WASTES

Their battle with the monster basilisk had taken a greater toll than they first realized. James and Sarah had escaped with mostly scratches and a few bruises, but Lusin's injuries were more serious. The punctures from the bite were shallow—thanks to his enchanted clothing—but the monster's venom had still entered his blood. A faint, dusky stain already traced a vein along his hip, like ink seeping through parchment.

James ignored his own exhaustion and insisted on tending to Lusin's wounds. He smeared crushed rue on strips of clean cloth and bound each injury with careful hands. The bitter, peppery scent of the herbs filled the air, cutting through the reek of rot that still drifted from the carcass behind them. As he worked, he tried not to think about how warm Lusin's skin felt—or how removing layers of clothing had revealed another patch of scales along the opposite hip. His fingers moved with the steady economy of training, but his pulse did not.

For one weak moment he gave in, brushing a fingertip lightly over the colorless scales as he tied a knot. They felt dry and impossibly smooth—almost slick—against his calloused finger. He wanted more. Lusin let out a tiny, involuntary gasp.

The sound went through him like a spark. James snatched his hand back. "Sorry," he muttered, eyes fixed on the bandages.

He could feel Lusin watching him. Heat rose to his cheeks, and he finished quickly before he could be tempted again. He also tried very hard not to dwell on how sensitive those scales must be—and how Lusin's gasp had nothing to do with pain. He smoothed the last strip of cloth and forced his hands to be practical, not curious.

"Finished," he mumbled, tugging Lusin's top back over the bandages and retreating—without looking like he was retreating—to gather the supplies. A mischievous chuckle froze him in place. Sarah had seen.

"Getting excited?" she asked, all wicked delight. James's face flamed. He refused to look back—at her or at Lusin, who was getting to his feet.

"W-What do you mean?" he stammered, pretending ignorance and failing spectacularly.

"You're hopeless," she teased, though her smile was softer than her words. The edge in her tone dulled into something like relief, as if teasing were easier than admitting how close they'd come.

"Shut up and help me find my blades," he snapped, desperate to change the subject. Sarah laughed lightly and came along to sift through the foul battlefield.

She found his sword quickly; the knife was more elusive. After what felt like forever, a glint in the sand snagged James's eye. He hurried toward it, only to find not his hunting knife—but the crystal compass. He hadn't realized he'd lost it during the fight. Now the stone burned as bright as the sun. Light pooled in its facets, steady and insistent.

Lusin joined him and took the necklace, studying the light.

"Does this mean what I think it means?" James asked, throat tight.

Lusin's gaze moved from the stone to the basilisk's carcass and back, confirming James's fear. "I'm afraid so. It seems the key is inside the body of the basilisk."

James groaned, then started stripping off his clothes. Sarah and Lusin stared.

"What? I'm not getting more of that slime on my clothes. I'd never get them clean." Sand clung to his skin immediately, and the sun pressed on already reddened skin.

Because fate hated them, the sun was high and merciless, cooking the desert and the corpse as they searched. Heat radiated off the blackened scales; flies discovered them in a dark, buzzing halo. Elbow-deep in reeking flesh, their effort began to feel futile. The texture was a catalogue of horrors—gristly bands, ruptured sacs of pus, the slick weight of organs that should never be named aloud.

"I'm never going to smell the same again!" James complained as the second hour bled by. Sweat ran into his eyes; he blinked through a sting that was only partly salt.

"Oh, shut up and keep looking," Sarah snapped. "It's got to be here somewhere."

He was too tired and dizzy to argue. He'd nearly died in battle—this endless scavenging was its own kind of hell. His arms shook with the work; his stomach rolled at each new pocket of gas that burped free and painted the air in death.

At last—just as he was certain he'd faint—his fingers closed around something small and hard. He shouted triumph and wrenched it free, holding it aloft. The metal flashed, miraculously clean where his hand had protected it.

He kicked himself out of the carcass and sprinted for the water, diving into the surf as clouds of black ichor lifted from his skin. The water was glorious. It folded around him, cool and sure, and peeled the stink away in ribbons. After a long, grateful moment, he scrubbed the object clean.

It looked almost like an ordinary brass key—ornate, abnormally heavy, with teeth on both sides and a single rich pearl set into the handle. A soft, steady glow pulsed within it, like a heartbeat. For all it had cost them, it felt impossibly small. He weighed it in his palm and felt the faintest hum, as if the thing recognized having been found.

Lusin appeared beside him, black blood streaked up his bare arms, staining his pale skin. The contrast made the lines of fatigue at the corners of his eyes starker.

"This has got to be it," James said, handing the key over.

"I believe you are right," Lusin murmured, turning it in his hand before passing it back. His fingers lingered at James's knuckles, a brief, steadying press.

"But why was it in that thing? I thought we had to find it and break a seal," James said.

Lusin frowned, then held up the compass. The crystal's light had gone dark, even with the key beside it. "The basilisk appears to have been a guardian. Perhaps slaying it and removing the key broke the seal."

"Are we going to have to do this every time?" James asked, dismayed.

"It is possible," Lusin said, eyes on the dead serpent. A new heaviness settled over them. The shore sounded louder for a moment, as if the sea had opinions about their chances.

They washed in knee-deep breakers without speaking. Salt stung the scrapes on James's arms; he welcomed the sting as proof of clean skin. James was rubbing the last of the grime from his fingers when he noticed Lusin staring at his right hand—expression calm, eyes strained.

"Lusin…?" James began, but Lusin stepped in and gently took his cursed hand, tracing the new lines with careful fingertips. They didn't hurt anymore—but they said everything about the time slipping away. The ink-dark branches had crept farther since morning; seeing them on the bright shore felt obscene.

"You will need to be more careful," Lusin murmured.

"Don't worry. We'll lift it in time," James said, putting more confidence into the words than he felt. Those golden eyes lifted to meet his. Worry softened to awe, then resolve. Lusin nodded. The hand around James's tightened once as if to seal a pact neither of them could name.

"If you two lovebirds are finished, we need to get going," Sarah called from the beach.

James glared over his shoulder.

"What does she mean, James? We are not birds," Lusin asked, earnest.

"Nothing. She's insane," James said quickly, slogging back to dress and break camp. Lusin tilted his head in confusion, then followed. He rolled the bandages and herb pouch with his usual neatness, even as fatigue dragged at the corners of his posture.

"We have to leave the Wastes immediately," Sarah said.

Their supplies were spread on the sand. They had maybe four days of food and water left if they rationed well—but the rue was the problem. After using it to treat Lusin, only one dose remained for both Sarah and James. That meant less than twenty-four hours to clear the poisoned land. It had taken three days to reach this point. The arithmetic was brutal and dispassionate.

"We could try going back to Radha," James said. "Maybe he has rue."

Sarah hesitated; the Serpent King's caverns were only a day's hard march away—but Lusin shook his head.

"Father doesn't keep any. I picked this for James while we were traveling."

James fell silent, thinking. He felt the map in his pack like a weight with edges.

"Maybe there's another way out. We just need to leave the Wastes, right?" he said, unrolling the map.

They were deep in the desert. The shortest path to the edge lay south—still a two-day trek without rest. The coast could shorten things, but they had nothing to build a raft. Every angle looked grim. Heat shimmered above the parchment; the inked dunes seemed to ripple like the real ones.

He scanned the shoreline. Red rocks. The twisted carcass. White sand. Turquoise water. The water was so clear he could see fish darting in the shallows—life, thriving. That had to mean it wasn't poisoned like the land.

"Hey, Lusin?" James asked. "If we reduce our exposure to the poisoned ground, would the rue last longer?"

Lusin considered. "It should," he said slowly. "How will you reduce your exposure?"

"The water. It doesn't look contaminated. We don't have a boat, but if we walk in the surf, maybe we can stretch the rue long enough to reach the edge."

Lusin nodded, unreadable. It was their only real chance. Two days was still two days.

"It's worth a try," Sarah said. "We should move." She turned south and stepped into the water. The surf took their calves with a cold that felt like mercy.

It was close. Far too close.

They'd walked three days. The last dose of rue had burned out twelve hours ago. Exhaustion and symptoms tightened their steps. Dizziness. Weakness. Confusion. Thoughts unspooled when they tried to braid them into plans. The sand seemed to tilt; the horizon breathed.

Finally—plants. The southern edge of the Wastes. Almost there.

Sarah was ghost-pale and panting, but still upright. James wasn't so lucky. Five hundred feet from salvation, he crumpled face-first into the surf. He felt too calm. He knew he could drown here. His body wouldn't move. The sea sounded like cloth torn slowly.

Strong arms grabbed him and lifted him from the water— Lusin's. Hot air gusted across his clammy skin as Lusin ran. Then the cool cushion of grass, and clean air. He smelled loam, crushed green, a sweetness that had nothing to do with desert wind.

Free of the Wastes—but breath still ragged. Fever raged. Somewhere in the fog, Sarah said something about it. Then darkness, drifting. Hot, cold. Voices over him, faces he half-recognized. Always, always Lusin—an anchor in the storm. Cool hands on his forehead, a cup at his lips, a voice saying his name in different shapes until one reached him.

Chirping woke him. Cheerful, ceaseless.

He blinked into a little room of warm wood and clean light. He lay in a soft bed beneath a cozy quilt. Across from him, the mirror of an old vanity with a pitcher and basin reflected a thinner, paler version of himself. To the left, a wide window spilled afternoon sun across ivory curtains that swayed in a cool breeze. The scent of flowers rode the air. Beyond the sill, green fields and rolling hills stretched away. Bees worried at something bright just outside; the sound was a soft, contented buzz.

He had never seen anything so peaceful—and had no idea how he'd gotten here.

A soft snore to his right made him jump. He turned, then nearly fell back against the pillows in relief.

Lusin slept in a wooden chair, head pillowed on crossed arms against the mattress. In the beam of light, his colorless skin glowed; his pastel hair haloed his face like spun moonlight. His fingers, relaxed at last, still curved as if remembering the shape of James's wrist.

Beautiful—but not restful. Fine lines of tension framed his mouth; shadows pooled under his eyes. Even asleep, he held himself like someone prepared to be needed at any second.

James's gaze flicked to the mirror again. His own reflection—gaunt, hollow-cheeked. He must have been unconscious for days. No wonder Lusin looked wrecked. The realization warmed something deep within him. Gratitude crowded his ribs until he had to breathe around it.

He couldn't help himself. Rolling to his side, he combed his fingers gently through Lusin's hair and ghosted his touch along his cheek. Soft as silk, cool as porcelain. He wished he could see the scales hidden by the angle of Lusin's face. He traced the air where he knew they would lie and felt foolish and happy at once.

A knock nearly launched him from the bed. Lusin stirred—either at the knock or James's jolt—and golden eyes blinked open. For a heartbeat, neither moved. Then wonder broke across Lusin's face.

"James!" he breathed, surging forward to gather him in his arms. His voice was rough with disuse. James hugged him back, overwhelmed. The embrace steadied the room; the world clicked into a truer place.

"Lusin?" A kind voice floated from the doorway. "I thought you might like a bite to eat. You'll be no use to Prince James when he wakes if you don't keep up your strength."

A plump older woman shouldered the door with a tray balanced in both hands. Her hair was cut close to her brow and was silver streaked with dark brown. Her round, friendly face matched her tone. When her watery green eyes found James awake, she paused—then smiled.

"Oh, Your Majesty! You're finally awake. I'll fetch more food," she said warmly.

"Yes, thank you," Lusin replied before James could speak. She nodded, set a plate of scrambled eggs at the foot of the bed, and turned to go. The steam curled up in pale ribbons; the smell made James suddenly, fiercely hungry.

"I'll bring Lady Sarah as well," she added, closing the door with a soft squeak.

James watched her go, then looked back at Lusin, who still had one hand on his shoulder and the other on his forearm. As much as he wanted to pull Lusin close again, one question burned through the haze.

"Lusin… how did I get here?"

Lusin's shoulders wilted. He looked down before answering. "You… wouldn't wake up," he said quietly. "We brought you here for help."

"James!!"

The door banged open as Sarah barreled into the room. She practically shoved Lusin aside and hauled James into a crushing hug. Lusin stepped back, face unreadable, while James wheezed in her grip.

"Sarah… I'm okay… let go," he rasped.

"I'm going to help get food," Lusin said tonelessly, slipping through the door. James stared after him. Lusin didn't do cold; he usually found Sarah's dramatics amusing.

"Don't worry about it," Sarah soothed, sensing James's confusion and releasing him. "You were out for a week. He took it really hard."

James swallowed. "Sarah… what happened?"

CHAPTER 16

FEVER

*O*ne week earlier, when the fever first began its grip, *Lusin had already felt the terror settling in his chest.*

Lusin's worry had sharpened into fear. Their rue was gone, the land ahead still endless, and James was fading with every step. From behind, he watched the prince stumble—his shoulders sagging, breath shallow. Sarah still held herself upright, steady as ever, and that only deepened his confusion. But James's eyes—bright, stubborn blue—still burned with resolve, and that flicker of strength kept Lusin moving.

When the green edge of the Wastes finally shimmered into view, relief surged through him. They were going to make it.

Without warning, James pitched forward into the shallow surf and didn't move. The splash was small—too small for the sound of a man collapsing.

"James!" Lusin dropped to his knees and pulled him from the water. The prince's chest heaved once—then again—but his eyes rolled back, his skin leaching to chalk. Panic hit Lusin like venom in his veins. He cradled James close, feeling the faint flutter of his pulse, and ran.

He ran until the world blurred. Every stride sent knives through his legs, but he didn't slow. The edge glowed ahead—green grass, safety, life. He burst across the border, collapsing to his knees amid the wet grass. They were out. They were safe. Or so he prayed.

Lusin laid James gently on the grass, but the stillness didn't break. Minutes dragged by. The prince's body trembled, sweat slicking his skin. His breath came in ragged bursts, and low, broken moans escaped him—sounds that clawed at Lusin's heart and soul.

Horror seized him. The venom—how could it still be spreading?

The Wastes were never empty. They were saturated.

Lusin had known that long before Radha ever named it. The land breathed basilisk venom the way forests breathed pollen. It clung to stone, rode the wind, settled into lungs and blood alike. That was why nothing grew. That was why travelers vanished. It was not a curse—it was accumulation.

Most bodies could endure it for a time. Strong ones longer.

James was not strong in that way.

The curse already gnawed at him, hollowing space where resilience should have lived. What the Wastes merely whispered into Sarah's blood, they poured into James's. Each breath here had been another drop added to a cup already too full.

He was watching James die. Sarah hovered nearby, helpless, eyes wide—and something ugly and hot flared inside Lusin. How dare she stand whole while his Sun withered?

Lusin did not think in terms of fairness. The world had never been fair to him, and he had never required it to be.

There was only what was his—and what was not.

James was his.

Everything else was incidental. Tools, obstacles, irritations. Sarah had always existed on that outer edge: tolerated because James reached for her, endured because removing her would cost him more than allowing her presence.

If James died, that tolerance would end. The thought settled with the same calm certainty as gravity.

A weak moan dragged him back to reality.

No. Anger was useless. He needed rue—needed it *now*. It was the only chance left.

"Lusin? Is he going to be okay?" Sarah's voice trembled as she spoke. He did not waste breath on her. Talking would only waste his precious time.

He scanned the horizon—lush grass, scattered trees, healthy soil. Rue could grow here. It *had* to.

"Lusin...?" Sarah's voice interrupted his thoughts for a second time. He looked at her and she recoiled as if he had struck her. As irritated as he was with her, she might have a use.

"Watch him. Do not let any harm come to him." He ordered her firmly. She kept quiet and nodded. Lusin ran his fingers through James's sweat-dampened hair and smoothed his thumb over his cheek, indulging himself for a second before he left. He had to be fast. Basilisk venom was potent and persistent, even in the strongest creatures.

Lusin searched in earnest and cursed himself as he went.

He had crossed worse lands than this.

He remembered taverns where men decided, foolishly, that fear was better replaced with bravado. He remembered the smell of blood on ale-soaked floors, remembered how quickly noise turned to silence when he stopped pretending to be harmless. Hunters had come for him too—armed, confident, already imagining the price of his head. They had been wrong. All of them.

None of that mattered now.

Violence was simple. This was not.

You could not cut poison out of the air. You could not intimidate a fever into retreat. All he could do was run and hope the earth still remembered how to heal.

He cursed himself for not picking more rue, for allowing Sarah to come, and for becoming careless and allowing himself to be bitten by the monster. If any one of those things had not happened, James would not be suffering right now from his people's venom.

The thought of his Sun's fragile state terrified him and his dread was threatening to overwhelm his mind. Only his determination to save James kept his mind clear enough to continue his search.

He ran until his lungs burned. When at last he spotted the yellow-flowered leaves, he ripped them from the ground, roots and all, and sprinted back.

James lay limp, breathing in shallow gasps. There was no time left. Lusin shoved the bitter weed into his own mouth and chewed. He chewed the rue until it turned thick and pulpy, then pressed his lips to James's and forced it between them, coaxing the prince's throat to swallow. When James obeyed, he nearly wept.

All he could do now was wait.

And wait he did. Time fractured.

Lusin counted breaths. When counting failed, he counted heartbeats. When even that slipped away, he watched James's chest rise and fall and anchored himself to the fact that it still moved.

He had held dying bodies before. He knew the signs. The way weight changed. The way warmth fled unevenly. The way hope tried to lie to you near the end.

He did not allow himself hope. He allowed vigilance.

Hours stretched into eternity, James's body hot in his arms, every shallow breath feeling too fragile. Sarah came and went as she pleased. She didn't dare try to speak again and he ignored her. His focus was completely on James, waiting patiently for him to open his eyes and shine once more.

The world was too dark without him. It made Lusin feel cold inside; a strange empty cold that had nothing to do with temperature. He had to believe James was going to be okay. All he had to do was be patient.

For a moment, hope dared to bloom—his breathing steadied, his color returned. But the fever came creeping soon after, burning brighter with every hour. It was long after sundown when Lusin knew something was very wrong. He looked around for Sarah and found her, perhaps twenty feet away. She had built a fire which was casting long shadows through the grass with its flickering light.

"Sarah..." He called in a warning voice. At once, she was kneeling beside them, her hands on James, feeling his wrists and his cheeks. She pressed her wrist against James's forehead while feeling her own at the same time. Lusin resisted the urge to pull James away from her searching hands. He allowed her to work but he couldn't help the prickling irritation he felt as she touched his Sun.

"His fever's too high," Sarah said, panic flickering in her eyes. "We need help—now." Immediately, she was on her feet. She rushed to gather her things and put out the fire with a snap of her fingers. Lusin stood, adjusting James in his arms as he did. His heart was pounding in his chest as he studied James's unresponsive face. They didn't have long. There had to be someone who could help him.

Lusin spread his magic like a net—conjuring serpent familiars and sending them through the grass, his mind riding with each. One by one, they found nothing. Then, finally, one whispered of a road. A light. Hope.

"This way!" he shouted, already running west. He didn't look back, trusting Sarah to handle herself. They ran beneath a bruised sky, the world a blur of silver grass and moonlight. James's fevered heat seared through Lusin's shirt, each moan driving him faster. He would not let death win. He kept reaching for the snake that was guiding him, its presence in the back of his mind comforting as it continually assured him that he was heading in the right direction.

At last—a light. A single candle in the dark, swaying in an iron lantern on a road like a promise. Carefully tended trees and fields next to a single-story farmhouse glowed with the weak silver light of the setting half moon. All the windows were dark.

Until this point, Lusin hadn't cared whether Sarah followed him or not. James was all that mattered to him but now, as they drew near the farmhouse, he realized she could have another use. He slowed his pace slightly and allowed Sarah to overtake him. Predictably, she ran straight for the door without slowing and started pounding on it while he stood back with James.

"Help! Please!" Sarah hammered at the door until her fists left dents. Inside, the sounds of muffled movement reached their ears and lights flickered awake, casting a warm glow into the cold night.

Slowly, the door creaked open and two people peered curiously through the gap. An old man of a medium build with a large salt-and-pepper handlebar mustache and matching bushy eyebrows stood at the front. He wore a thin white shirt with suspenders and stood just in front of an old woman, whom Lusin assumed to be the man's wife. She was plump and wore what looked like a white and floral nightgown and in her left hand, she held high a lit candle. She peered over her husband's shoulder with curious pale green eyes as she adjusted her spectacles with her free hand.

"What's going on here?" The old man demanded.

"Please! It's my brother. He is very sick and we have no way to help him." Sarah pleaded as tears spilled from her eyes. As one, the farmer and his wife turned to look at James and Lusin. Their eyes studied James's unresponsive body in his arms, then they passed over Lusin's face and lingered on his cheek.

In that horrifying moment, he realized he had forgotten to cover his head. Their eyes widened simultaneously as recognition came to them. He had seen that look before—usually moments before someone decided to try their luck. Predictably, fear entered them and they looked back at Sarah.

"Young lady, do you even know what that *thing* is?!" the farmer barked, pointing a crooked finger at Lusin. He felt his muscles coil as he took note of Sarah's position and his own distance from the door, ready to flee with James if he must.

Sarah stood her ground. "He's my friend. Please—help my brother!" She begged. The man scowled but his wife was staring at Lusin, her eyes full of what looked like pity.

"Please..." Lusin said in a low voice while looking down at James's face flushed with fever. He could feel all eyes turn to him, "Please... save him." He had never begged for anything before in his life but he would do that and anything else if it would save James's life. He glanced up to see that the old man still looked suspicious but his wife shouldered past him and hurried to Lusin. She clicked her tongue as she felt James's heated forehead and checked the pulse in his neck.

"Oh, poor boy. He really isn't doing well, is he? Let's get him inside and take a better look." Her voice was as kind as her round face. She turned and shuffled back to the house, expecting him to follow but Lusin stared after her. Other than James, no one had shown him such kindness after they knew what he was.

The old lady paused at the door and looked over her shoulder back at him, "Well, are you coming, young man? We need to get your friend inside." Lusin nodded and hurried to follow.

She ushered them through a narrow hall to a cozy guest room. "Lay him there," she ordered, pointing to the bed.

When she tried to send him out, Lusin's stare made her pause. After a heartbeat, she sighed. "Fine. Stay. You can help. It wouldn't hurt to have another pair of hands." She conceded before turning to her husband and Sarah, "As for the rest of you, out! I will tell you how he's doing and let you see your brother later but for now, I need room to work." She shooed them out the door and shut it after them.

Then, she gestured to a wooden chair that was sitting beside the bed, "You will sit there when you are not helping me." She rummaged in the drawers of a vanity set at the foot of the bed and pulled out what looked like clean rags and a jar of herbs, "For now, you will make yourself useful and hold this."

*

Three days passed in a haze of candlelight and worry.

Lusin never left James's side. He learned to crush herbs, measure tinctures, and trust the quiet old woman whose hands worked like gentle clockwork. Slowly, James began to mend. At the end of the third day, they were giving James his daily medicine when the old woman surprised Lusin by speaking.

"This boy isn't her brother, is he?" she said at last, eyes sharp. It was more a statement of fact than a question. Lusin stared at her and she returned his look with one of her own. He decided there was no point in lying to the person who was saving James's life. He honestly still wasn't sure why Sarah had told them that at all.

He shook his head 'no'. She looked satisfied as she went back to work. "I thought not. They look nothing alike." They worked in renewed silence. When they had finished and she was smoothing the quilt over James's chest, she suddenly ran her fingers through James's hair and looked to be examining it. Then she spoke again.

"He's Prince James," she added softly. "And you—you're a basilisk." She looked to Lusin for an answer and he responded with a nod. She hummed and went back to excessively smoothing the blankets. Lusin was curious why she would make such a statement when she already knew that he was.

Still, he nodded a second time. "A strange place the world has become when a Prince shows up dying on your doorstep accompanied by a girl and a deadly serpent." She mused more to herself than to the world at large. Lusin kept his peace and watched her fidgeting until she was standing beside him. "Well, he's not quite out of the woods yet, but he is responding well to his treatments." She finished obsessively smoothing the wrinkles from the blanket then turned and took one of his scaled hands in both of her own.

"He's going to be fine," she said with a smile. "You did well, dear."

The weight on Lusin's chest dissolved. James would live. Suddenly, the image of her face started to swim and his cheeks felt wet. He touched his fingers to his face and saw that they came back damp with tears. The sensation baffled him. His body was leaking warmth where none should exist. The woman's smile grew warmer as she watched his bewilderment.

"There, there," the woman said kindly, patting his scaled hand. "No need for that." He looked away and wiped his face with his sleeve.

"Thank you." He whispered. She rubbed his fingers again in that way that was oddly comforting.

"What is your name, dear? I simply must know the name of the boy who loves the prince so."

"Lusin."

CHAPTER 17
JEALOUSY

It was a long moment before Sarah answered James. He still felt weak, his muscles tender from days of disuse, but relief kept him sitting upright despite the weight pressing down on his limbs. The quiet stretched so long that he began to think she hadn't heard him at all. He opened his mouth to ask again, struggling for breath—but she spoke first.

"You collapsed before we got out of the Wastes," she said, her voice trembling like a plucked string.

James tried to gather the scattered fragments of memory. The heat had pressed on him like a living thing, the air turning to syrup in his lungs, every heartbeat echoing in his ears. He remembered the world tilting, the sky spinning, then crashing water and darkness swallowing everything. After that—nothing but drifting void and the occasional muffled voice.

"Lusin carried you out," Sarah continued. "We thought you'd recover—like I did once we were clear—but… you didn't."

Her posture stiffened. She stared at the floor, black eyes shining with trapped tears. "You wouldn't wake up. You burned with fever. We went looking for help and found this place. We barely made it in time, James." His name broke on her tongue like glass.

James blinked, stunned. He made a mental note to thank the couple who had taken them in—kind strangers who had opened their home to travelers who didn't look safe or easy to approach. They had saved his life.

Fat tears splattered onto the wooden floor. Sarah covered her mouth with both hands as if embarrassed by the sound of her own ragged sobs. Her shoulders curled inward. For a moment she looked smaller than he'd ever seen her.

James stared. He had seen her furious, cynical, grief-stricken, even panicked—but never broken. Sarah was a force of nature. She didn't cry; she *caused* crying in others. Yet here she was, shaking apart because of him.

"It's okay, Sarah. I'm okay now—" he began, unsure how to comfort her, unsure if she'd let him.

"We thought you were going to *DIE!*" she burst out suddenly, her voice sharp and raw. She slammed a fist into the mattress hard enough to make the frame creak, then collapsed over her knees, sobbing so violently her breath came in shuddering gasps.

James hesitated, then reached out. He caught her wrist and tugged her gently to sit beside him. She didn't resist—just dropped heavily onto the edge of the bed, trembling. He wrapped an arm around her shoulders. She hid her face against his shoulder, tears soaking into his shirt. He rubbed her arm slowly, trying to anchor her while his own head spun with exhaustion.

When her sobs softened, her breathing still uneven, he murmured, "I'm sorry, Sarah. I didn't mean to put you through that."

"I did better than Lusin," she sniffled, wiping her face on her sleeve. "We couldn't make him leave your side. He wouldn't eat or sleep. He didn't speak. I started worrying about him as much as you!"

She gave a watery laugh, half-hysterical from relief. James couldn't help but laugh back, though softly.

"I'm glad you're finally warming up to him," he teased weakly. She elbowed him, but lightly.

"Shut up," she muttered, though her lips twitched. She sniffed again. "He really cares about you."

James's breath hitched. Heat crept up the back of his neck. He tried to look casual but failed miserably. "You really think so?" he asked, barely above a whisper.

Sarah turned and stared at him like he'd announced the sky was sometimes blue. "James, I will never understand how someone can be so brilliant and so hopelessly dense at the same time."

He made a wounded noise. She ignored it.

"And it's obvious you're just as gone for him," she added smugly.

He rolled his eyes but didn't deny it, which only made her smirk harder.

Before he could get out a defense—or slip into full meltdown—the door creaked open.

Lusin stood in the doorway, a tray balanced carefully in his hands: stew, bread, and a pitcher of clear water. The warm scent drifted into the room. The door closed behind him with a soft click that felt far too loud.

His eyes found James first—relief flickering through the gold—but then drifted to Sarah sitting close beside him. Close enough that her thigh touched his. Close enough that James's arm still circled her shoulders. Lusin froze mid-step.

There was no dramatic gasp, no hiss, no violence. Just a flicker.

Quick as lightning. Sharp as a blade.

Jealousy.

James yanked his arm away from Sarah so fast he nearly elbowed her in the ribs. Too late.

It took Sarah longer to put the pieces together. When understanding finally dawned, she went rigid, turning the exact color of overheated iron. Then—

"Lusin! Thank you for bringing James some food!" she squeaked, her voice pitching several humiliating octaves higher than usual.

Lusin said nothing. He simply watched her with an expression perfectly polite—and perfectly terrifying.

Sarah squeezed herself along the wall, trying to slide around him toward the door. It was like watching someone attempt to escape a dragon's hoard without disturbing the gold.

"I'm sure you two have a lot to talk about so I'll just be leaving now," she babbled in a single breath as she struggled to open the door.

The latch finally surrendered. She disappeared through the gap like a startled squirrel. The door shut behind her with a soft thump.

Silence fell. A deep, thick, syrupy silence that weighed on James's chest.

Lusin remained facing the door a moment longer, the muscles in his back tense as bowstrings. Then he turned and crossed the room quietly. He sat beside James—so close the mattress dipped, so close James could feel the faint warmth radiating beneath the coolness of his skin.

Without a word, Lusin settled the tray across James's lap. He took the spoon, dipped it into the stew, and lifted it toward James's mouth.

"Lusin, really, I can—" James began, embarrassed.

But Lusin's eyes were soft. Almost pleading. He looked like someone who needed something to do, something to prove, something to anchor himself to reality. James swallowed the protest.

He opened his mouth. Accepted the bite.

Lusin fed him in silence: spoonful after spoonful, slow and careful. James barely tasted the food. His gaze kept catching on the dark smudges under Lusin's eyes, the hollowed cheeks, the faint tremor in his fingers. He looked exhausted, more exhausted than James had ever seen him.

He looked haunted.

"I'm sorry, Lusin," James whispered.

Lusin paused mid-motion. "I don't understand, James. Why are you apologizing?" His voice was thin and low. "None of this was your doing."

"I just… feel bad for worrying you."

Lusin lowered his gaze to the bowl. "You are well now. That is all that matters."

When the last spoonful was gone, James sagged against the pillows. Lusin placed the tray aside and tugged the quilt up around him, smoothing the fabric with gentle, almost reverent hands. His eyes drifted to the marks on James's right hand.

The mask slipped.

"It's okay, Lusin," James murmured. "We have time."

The basilisk took his hand gently, as if afraid it might break. His cool fingertips traced the darkening branches of the curse.

"It's spreading," he whispered.

James tried to smile. "Just a little. Your father said it has to cover my whole body before it takes effect. We've got plenty of time."

Lusin didn't look convinced. "Sarah did not succumb to the poison as you did. I believe the curse is draining your strength faster than we realized."

James frowned but didn't argue. The stew warmed his stomach, the soft pillow supported his head, and the room felt safe—almost like being home. His eyelids drooped.

He felt Lusin's hand tighten around his own.

"Rest, James. I will be here when you wake," Lusin whispered.

James tried to say thank you, but the words dissolved. As he slipped under, he thought—just for a heartbeat—that he felt cool fingers brush his cheek... and the ghost of lips against his own.

He wasn't sure if it was real.

He hoped it was.

CHAPTER 18
JAMES AND LUSIN

James didn't know how long he had been asleep, but when the darkness finally lifted, he woke to nearly the same scene as before. The only real difference was that this time, Lusin was awake. Once again, the serpent prince tended quietly to his needs—adjusting blankets, refreshing the cool cloth on his forehead, watching him with that focused, unwavering attention that made James's heart beat both faster and painfully slower.

By late afternoon, however, James was starting to feel caged. Being still too long made him restless. He had spent most of his life with tutors, obligations, and the constant pressure of expectation—he wasn't built for lying around unless he was genuinely unconscious.

"James, I don't think it's a good idea for you to move so much," Lusin cautioned as James threw back the quilt and swung his legs over the bed. His brow pinched slightly, a small crease of worry etched just above the bridge of his nose.

"I'm fine, Lusin. I just want to look around a bit." The room felt too small, too quiet, too full of unspoken things. He needed air. He planted both feet on the smooth wooden floor, stood—and promptly collapsed as his legs buckled, refusing to support even his pride.

Lusin caught him instantly, his arms firm and steady as James slumped against his chest instead of the ground. The basilisk gave him a knowing look—one that said *I told you so* without uttering a word. James just grinned sheepishly, because truly, what else could he do?

"Thanks, Lusin! Help me through the door, will you?"

Lusin looked like he wanted to refuse, but James widened his smile, knowing full well the prince wouldn't be able to resist him for long. It was embarrassingly effective. Without another word, Lusin sighed—soft and resigned—and adjusted his grip, wrapping one strong arm around James's waist. James leaned into him more than strictly necessary, feeling the cool, steady strength of him as they crossed the threshold.

The short hall opened into a large, warm room that looked like something out of a dream. A long polished table stood at the center, resting atop a richly patterned floral rug. The walls were a mix of sturdy wood and stone, and a huge hearth dominated the left wall. A lively fire crackled inside, painting the room in amber light. The scent of cooking stew, herbs, and freshly baked bread floated through the air.

Glass jars, bundles of dried flowers, and carefully folded quilts filled the shelves in an organized jumble that radiated comfort. James inhaled deeply, surprised at how soothing it all felt. So different from the cold marble of the palace or the dark grandeur of the Serpent King's caverns. This place was warmth made tangible.

An elderly man sat at the far end of the table, his elbow propped casually on the wood. Bald on top, with a magnificent salt-and-pepper handlebar mustache, he looked like someone carved out of sturdy oak and stubbornness. His eyebrows were so bushy they nearly shadowed his eyes, and his hands were broad and calloused—marks of a lifetime of fields and storms.

Sarah sat beside him, hat tossed on the table, chatting animatedly. The two were so engrossed in their conversation that neither noticed James's entrance at first. The old woman bustled between the stove and counter, humming softly to herself as she wiped down surfaces that were already spotless.

When she spotted him, she gasped. "Your Majesty!" she exclaimed, wiping her hands on her apron as she hurried over. "Are you sure you should be up so soon?"

"I'm okay, really. And please—call me James." He tried not to wince as his legs trembled under him.

Her fussing drew Sarah's attention. The young mage turned, froze, and shot to her feet like she'd been lit on fire. "James, you idiot! What do you think you're doing?!"

"Relax, Sarah," he said with an exaggerated roll of his eyes. "I just got bored and wanted to look around."

Truthfully, hearing her yell again settled something inside him. The quiet worry in her earlier voice had been too unsettling. Sarah was many things, but quiet was not one of them.

"Don't you feel the least bit bad about using poor Lusin as your personal crutch?" she demanded, gesturing accusingly at the basilisk.

James opened his mouth, but before he could answer, Lusin's arm tightened around his waist—subtle but protective. James glanced up just in time to catch the sharp look the basilisk shot at Sarah—colder than he'd ever seen from him. Sarah blinked, taken aback.

Without a word, Lusin maneuvered James toward the back door and out into the cool evening air.

Outside, the world felt wide again. Lusin guided him carefully to a low stone wall. He eased James down onto it, hands gentle but precise. Then he stepped back, his face unreadable in the soft twilight, before turning so James could no longer see his face.

The silence that followed felt tense. The sky was painted in streaks of violet and fading gold. A gentle breeze lifted, attempting to fill the void with its whisper. James adjusted himself uncomfortably as he waited for Lusin to break the silence.

"You're upset," Lusin said at last, voice calm but distant—like he was bracing for something.

James blinked. Maybe Sarah was right—he *really* was easy to read.

"Not upset," James said gently. "Just wondering what's wrong."

Lusin stood still as carved jade, the faint breeze ruffling the pale strands of his hair. Time stretched between them, long and fragile. Finally, Lusin spoke.

"I'm sorry, James."

"For what?"

A long pause. Then: "I was rude to Sarah."

James blinked, then chuckled. "Oh, that? You don't have anything to apologize for. I was just surprised, that's all. She usually doesn't get under your skin."

Lusin hesitated. His voice, when it came, was quiet— barely above the whispering grass. "I did not realize you two were so... close."

Ah. There it was.

"Yeah," James said with a laugh. "We grew up together. We fight a lot, but we also really care about each other."

Lusin turned to him then. A faint smile curved his lips, though it didn't quite reach his eyes. "I'm glad you have someone you care about... who cares so much about you."

Something in his tone—soft, wounded, resigned—made James's breath catch.

"Lusin, what's going on? You... you almost sound like you're saying goodbye."

The basilisk didn't respond. His golden eyes held something deep and difficult—longing, pain, and a quiet sort of despair. James's panic rose like a tide.

"Lusin," he said softly, "you know Sarah and I don't like each other like *that*, right?"

Lusin blinked. Confusion flickered, replacing the sorrow. "Like… that?"

"You know," James said awkwardly, gesturing vaguely between them, "We aren't interested in each other… romantically."

The shift was immediate—and visible. Tension drained from Lusin's posture like water from cupped hands. Slowly, warmth returned to his eyes. Then came that heart-melting, squinty little smile James hadn't seen since before the Wastes.

Relief flooded the air around them. James found himself mirroring Lusin's smile.

"Come sit with me," he said, patting the wall beside him.

Lusin obeyed without hesitation. He sat close—close enough that their shoulders brushed. Close enough that James could feel his warmth through the cool evening air.

For a heartbeat, James hesitated. Then he gave in. He wrapped an arm around Lusin's shoulders, pulling him gently against his side. Lusin leaned in with quiet trust, resting lightly against him. James's heart swelled until it felt almost painful.

They sat together in silence as twilight deepened. Stars kindled across the sky one by one. The crescent moon was a perfect silver curve above them.

James looked down. Lusin's head rested on his shoulder, his fine scales catching the moonlight like faint frost. The sight made James's stomach flip, warm and sweet.

"The moon is beautiful tonight," James whispered, hoping that his pale companion would understand.

Lusin lifted his head. His golden eyes locked onto James's—soft, luminous, filled with wonder.

James reached up, brushing his fingers along Lusin's cheek. The scales there were smooth and cool beneath his thumb, shifting subtly as though alive under his touch. Lusin's eyes fluttered closed. A soft humming breath escaped him, almost a purr, as he leaned into James's hand.

Then Lusin covered James's hand with his own, pressing his cheek into his palm. He inhaled deeply—as though memorizing him, absorbing him.

When he opened his eyes again, they glowed with open, unguarded adoration.

James's heart thundered. Slowly, he cupped Lusin's chin, lifting it gently, leaning in—

Then—

"Boys? It's time for dinner!"

The kindly old woman's voice shattered the moment like a dropped plate.

James practically leapt out of his own skin, flailing embarrassingly before falling back against Lusin's chest. Lusin laughed softly—quiet and amused.

"Oh—okay," James called back, voice cracking as he tried to recover. "Thank you, we'll be in shortly."

She nodded and retreated inside.

James exhaled, pressing a hand to his face. His heart raced violently. His cheeks felt hot enough to light a campfire. "Do you know her name, Lusin? I really don't want to keep calling her 'the old lady.'"

Lusin steadied him as he stood. "I don't know her name. She told me to call her… Grandma."

James nearly tripped over a pebble. "Grandma," he repeated, trying not to smile too hard. "Of course she did."

Together, they walked inside—Lusin's arm still firmly around his waist.

CHAPTER 19
THE DELTA SWAMPS

It took another three days before Sarah and Lusin agreed James was strong enough to travel. To James, every hour of enforced rest felt like a personal insult. He didn't *feel* sick; he didn't feel weak; he didn't even feel tired. What he felt was trapped.

Every time he so much as shifted on the bed, one of them materialized at his side like a concerned shadow. He knew they meant well—Sarah with her clipped reminders about healing time, Lusin with his gentle but unyielding attentiveness—but the constant fussing left him exasperated.

Still, he complied. It wasn't worth fighting over something that would only earn him more hovering. Lusin kept a quiet, steady presence near him at all hours, tending to anything James claimed he could do himself.

Sarah assisted Grandma with preparing his food and medicines, measuring out portions like she expected him to crumble if he ate wrong. James hated feeling like an invalid, but he reminded himself again and again that it wouldn't last forever. Healing was temporary. Resentment didn't need to be.

On the evening of the third day, the three of them gathered around the polished dinner table, Radha's map spread between their hands. Candlelight flickered against the parchment as they leaned over the regions ahead.

"It looks like the key in the Delta Swamps is closest," Sarah said.

"Yeah, it does," James agreed. "We'll have to be very careful traveling there."

He tried to keep his tone even, but the truth prickled behind his ribs. He'd grown up hearing the kinds of stories no child should hear before bed—tales of the Swamps swallowing people whole, of lights dangling in the distance to lure travelers into pools of black water, of things beneath the surface that whispered. Even now, he could picture the illustrations from old books: skeletal trees, endless fog, water that never reflected the sky. And whether the stories were exaggerated or not, nobody had ever spoken of the place fondly.

But logic didn't care about his feelings. The two other keys were much farther in opposite directions: the far western border in the Estredan Mountains and the northern edge of the Range of Fire. The Swamps came next, whether he liked it or not.

They left at dawn the following morning. James thanked Grandma and Grandpa repeatedly, promising compensation when he returned. They brushed it off with warm, earnest pride.

"Knowing we helped our dear prince is all the reward we need," Grandma said. "We were able to repay King Alfred for all he's done for us."

James smiled and thanked her again, though a quiet stubbornness flared beneath his gratitude. He refused to leave such kindness unpaid. Before they left, he placed much of his gold on the bed he'd recovered in. He imagined them finding it later—Grandma's gasp, Grandpa shaking his head while smiling—and it softened the guilt of leaving yet another family concerned on his behalf.

Compared to the Wastes, traveling through the Neva Hills felt like stepping into a memory of peace. The sun warmed instead of burned. Grass rolled in soft waves, rich and green. Trees were full, their shadows dappled. At night, the air stayed mild, fireflies drifting through the dark like tiny lanterns guiding them forward. The quiet beauty tugged at something deep inside James. Only three weeks had passed since he and Lusin had traveled alone through landscapes like this, but it felt like it had been in another lifetime.

The people they met along the way treated them with friendly curiosity. Living so close to the Wastes, they recognized what Lusin was instantly, and more than once they used James's illusion spell to avoid unwelcome attention. The spell drained him, tugged at the edges of his strength, but he never complained. For Lusin, he would have done much more.

After everything they'd survived, James felt a sharper protectiveness toward the serpent prince than before. They hadn't discussed the almost-kiss, but something between them had shifted. Their closeness came easier now—fingers brushing, hands clasping without hesitation, small touches exchanged without thought. Sarah teased less and smiled more when she caught them.

By the fourth day, the land began to change. The air thickened, carrying moisture James could feel clinging to his skin. Tall grasses grew patchy. Trees darkened from comforting brown to cold gray. Every shift was subtle, but the accumulation was undeniable: they were entering a different world.

On the fifth day, they reached the lip of a shallow lake of black water. Lily pads floated like old coins while reeds bowed and frayed. Farther in, skeletal trees rose like dark monuments, their gray moss dangling in veils. The water was so still it reminded James of glass—unbroken, depthless, watching. Even the "logs" half-submerged in clustered shadows seemed wrong, as though they were waiting.

The sunlight dimmed beneath a heavy, milky sky, stealing cheer as it went. Everything smelled of stagnant water, mud, algae, and rot. The mud beneath their boots shifted from firm earth to something slick and pulsing with moisture. Fog curled low over the water, moving slowly, like breath from a sleeping giant.

Heat pressed down on them like a damp blanket. Sweat clung to James's skin until he was soaked through. Every step felt heavier, as though the Swamps themselves objected to their presence.

Wetlands and shallow lakes forced them to backtrack repeatedly. A path that looked promising would dissolve into open water twenty steps later. The ground sloped unpredictably; mud sucked at their boots so often James lost count of how many times he nearly toppled.

By sunset they faced an uncomfortable truth: there was no dry ground to pitch a camp. Their feet throbbed. Their clothes clung. Their tempers frayed. When they finally found a damp-but-not-flooded patch of grass, exhaustion pushed them to settle.

Everything around them was wet—grass, bark, air, breath. The wood they gathered was so waterlogged it refused to catch, even when stacked like a pyre. In the end, Sarah conjured a fire large enough to hold back the cold, the damp, and the army of biting insects.

It was still miserable. The ground seeped chill into their bones. Humidity clung to their blankets. Mosquitoes sounded like tiny blades slicing the air.

James huddled under his coverings, shivering. The fire warmed his face but couldn't chase the cold gripping his spine. Beside him, Lusin stayed rigid, alert, his gaze fixed on the black water as though something might rise from it at any moment. His seriousness unsettled James more than the swamps themselves.

At one point, James swore he saw a pair of pale orbs floating just above the shallows. They reflected the firelight—then slipped silently beneath the surface. He blinked hard, unsure if it was exhaustion or warning. Sleep came eventually, but it was thin and restless.

"James." Lusin's hand on his shoulder pulled him up from foggy dreams. Everything was wet—blanket, hair, breath. Across the fire's remains, Sarah blinked sleepily.

"Lusin? What is it? What's wrong?" James muttered, still groggy.

"We need to start moving," was all Lusin said.

James rose without argument.

The day looked exactly the same as the one before—white sky, thick heat, mist moving like a curtain. Time dissolved into the oppressive atmosphere. Sweat poured down James's back within minutes. His boots squished with every step, and even the act of lifting his hand to swat a mosquito felt like unnecessary labor.

"How much farther to Dorchas? We should have arrived by now," he muttered, slapping at the newest bite blooming on his neck.

"All that backtracking cost us time," Sarah replied sharply. "We should see it before sundown."

"I hope so. I can't take another night out here. I want a real bed." Sarah only nodded, too drained to offer her usual sarcasm.

James glanced at Lusin. The serpent prince was coated in mud and sweat, but his movements remained precise and alert. His eyes scanned the trees and water with unwavering focus. The tension radiating off him tightened something deep in James's chest. Lusin wasn't just cautious—he was anticipating something.

They walked for hours. The silence was as stifling as the air and both were never-ending. James started to feel like his sanity was slipping. Every bend looked identical. Every patch of ground looked like a repeat of the last ten. He began to wonder if he had died in the night and had been damned to wander this road to nowhere for all eternity.

Then, finally—light.

A single orange glow flickered in the distance, faint but unmistakable. Relief surged through James like he'd been underwater and finally surfaced. He quickened his pace.

As they approached, the scene unfolded into something eerie and surreal. A tall black iron lamp stood alone at the edge of a massive black lake. Its glass glowed a soft, steady orange, casting long reflections across the water. The lake was so still it mirrored the lamp with perfect clarity, as though the world above and below were twins.

To the left, a small white boat floated motionless, untethered yet completely still. To the right, a weathered sign leaned in the mud: Dorchas.

James slowed. Sarah froze. Lusin moved ahead, arm raised to bar James protectively.

Someone stood in the boat.

A hooded figure, tall and broad, faced away from them. A long black cloak draped to his boots. He gripped a tall staff or pole with both hands, head bowed. He looked carved from shadow. The boat didn't sway or bob beneath him—not even slightly.

James swallowed, unsure if calling out was wise. He glanced at Lusin, whose eyes were locked on the boatman with an unreadable expression. A long minute stretched thin.

Then the cloak rippled in a nonexistent breeze.

"Now, young ones," a gruff voice rasped across the water, "don't try an old man's patience. Do you wish to go to Dorchas, or not?"

The man turned his hooded head. His face was mostly hidden, but his pale skin and full white mustache and beard were visible in the lamplight. His eyes glimmered faintly from the shadows. James felt the hair on his neck rise.

"Um… yes. Is it far?" he asked.

"No. Not far."

The old man turned to face them properly and straightened, revealing a thin, angular face carved from hardship—high cheekbones, deep-set hollows, an expression that seemed incapable of warmth. Only his eyes shone with their own light like gray stars, sharp and cold. Regret coiled low in James's stomach, but stepping back now felt worse than moving forward.

"H-how much… to cross?" he asked.

"For the three of you, a gold coin should suffice."

Steep, but reasonable if it meant moving on—or at least, that was what James told himself. He had started this; he would finish it. He stepped forward, ignoring Lusin's tension at his back.

The boatman extended his palm. His fingers were bony and cold. James placed the coin into that skeletal hand. The old man bit it, tugged once, then smiled, showing crooked brown teeth.

"Climb aboard. I will take you to Dorchas."

James glanced back. Lusin gave a small, firm nod. Sarah's expression was horrified, eyebrows high, mouth tense—but she didn't argue. James inhaled, squared his shoulders, and stepped forward.

Lusin moved in front of him and boarded first, scanning every inch of the boat as though expecting it to attack. Then he helped James down and instantly positioned himself between

James and the boatman. James gripped Sarah's hand and helped her aboard opposite them. Her expression screamed, *What have you done?* He pretended not to notice.

Lusin's hand found his. Steady, grounding. James squeezed back.

The boat turned away from the shore without a sound.

It glided across the still water, carrying them deeper into the dark.

CHAPTER 20

DORCHAS,
THE CITY OF ETERNAL NIGHT

The boat slipped soundlessly across the glassy lake, the orange glow of the lamplight shrinking behind them until it was swallowed by fog. The water didn't even ripple as they moved, as though the lake refused to acknowledge their presence. Only the quiet rhythm of the pole striking the surface marked their passage toward Dorchas, each tap echoing too sharply in the suffocating dark.

All remaining light faded to nothingness, yet still they went on—gliding silently across the black water. The darkness thickened like a living thing, pressing against their faces and stealing the breath from their lungs. Not even the faintest glimmer of starlight pierced the sky; it was as if the heavens themselves had been erased. James raised a hand experimentally and saw absolutely nothing—only felt the cold air brush his fingertips.

At first, he was confident. Even excited. They had a destination, a guide (kind of), and no visible danger. But the deeper they slipped into this void, the more that confidence shriveled. The absence of sound was wrong. Even in forests at night, there were insects and distant animals and the whisper of wind. Here, nothing stirred except the water tapped by the ferryman's pole. James kept his face turned forward, gripping Lusin's hand tightly, as if the serpent prince were the last anchor preventing him from drifting into madness.

The darkness and silence pressed down on him until his skin crawled. He resisted the urge to twist around, terrified that if he looked back, he would see the boatman's glimmering gray-star eyes inches from his face. His thoughts spiraled—had they made a mistake trusting a stranger in a place like this? Did this lake even have an end? Could they already be drifting in circles, lost forever in some eternal pocket of night?

As time stretched on, dread rose in his chest like a tide. The trip felt endless. He squeezed Lusin's hand until his knuckles ached, inching backward until his spine touched Lusin's chest. The warmth there steadied him more than anything else. Embarrassed or not, he couldn't make himself care. He needed something real. Something warm. Something *alive*.

Lusin returned the gesture without hesitation, his arms sliding securely around James's middle. The serpent prince rested his chin on James's shoulder, breath warm despite the chill. The gentle exhale against his ear sent shivers down James's spine, fear mixing with comfort in a dizzying blend.

"It's okay, James. I am here," Lusin whispered.

The simple words cracked through the suffocating darkness like a lantern flame. James placed his free hand over Lusin's, grounding himself. For a few breaths, he simply let himself be held, tucked safely in Lusin's arms, hidden from sight within the endless void. Suspended in the dark, the world felt impossibly small—just the two of them and the faint creak of the boat.

Then, out in the distance, a faint orange glow winked into existence.

James blinked hard, uncertain if his mind had conjured it. But slowly, more pinpricks of light formed—faint, fragile, floating above the water. They shimmered through the mist, swelling one by one until they resembled lanterns drifting in a slow, deliberate dance across the horizon.

James leaned forward in awe, releasing his death grip on Lusin. The pale prince's arm tightened instinctively, anchoring him as he craned his neck toward the luminescent horizon. A soft gasp left James's lips as the lights multiplied, turning the distant fog a soft, warm orange.

One by one, lopsided silhouettes emerged—shapes of crooked buildings appearing as if pulled from another world. Rough wooden shacks sat on raised platforms ten or fifteen feet above the lake's surface, arranged in disorganized clusters. The fog thinned around them as if afraid to touch the lights, revealing walkways suspended above the water like a web of decaying planks.

Their small vessel slid alongside a warped dock framed between two iron lamps. As James climbed out, the creaking boards groaned beneath his boots, sounding alarmingly unstable. He turned to thank the boatman—

—and froze.

The boat was empty.

"Where did he go?!" James yelped, nearly pitching himself backward into the water in his panic.

Lusin caught him by the shoulders, grounding him long enough for his heart to stop sprinting.

"James! Keep your voice down—we should at least try to blend in." Sarah's sharp whisper cut through his alarm like a knife.

"But he's gone! He was right there, and now—he's just gone!" James babbled, pointing frantically while clinging to Lusin.

"I'm not surprised," Sarah muttered with an eye-roll so dramatic it nearly made a sound. "I've come to accept that anything is possible while following your dumb ass around. Come on—we need to find an inn."

She turned toward a narrow staircase of splintered planks angling upward. James scowled after her, cheeks burning, then reluctantly followed with Lusin close behind.

At the top of the stairs, James stopped short.

Dorchas stretched before them like a dream warped at the edges. The wooden platforms forming the "streets" were uneven, mismatched, and slick with moisture, some rising slightly higher than others as though the entire city shifted over time. Buildings leaned precariously on stilts, propped against each other like drunkards for stability. Wrought-iron lamps cast yellow-orange pools of light into the darkness, revealing little beyond their immediate reach.

Crooked signs swung lazily in the stagnant air, their painted letters faded or peeling. Moth-eaten curtains billowed from open windows despite the absence of wind, their ghostly motion sending a chill down James's spine. The entire city looked cobbled together from remnants scavenged from forgotten worlds—jury-rigged, waterlogged, and desperate to stay standing.

Above and below, there was nothing—no stars, no moon, no horizon. Only blackness swallowing the edges of the light.

Without prompting, Sarah and Lusin pulled their hoods up. James hesitated, thinking briefly about using the illusion spell for Lusin again, but the tingling in his cursed arm had been growing steadily worse all day. His strength was unreliable at best.

Sarah elbowed him sharply. "Put on your hood, you idiot," she hissed.

"Yeah, yeah," he grumbled, tugging it up over his golden hair. But once he looked around—seeing every cloaked figure moving like silent shadows—he understood her urgency.

Despite the number of people moving through the streets, Dorchas was eerily quiet. No laughter. No music. No smells of celebration or life. Only the creak of boards and the soft murmur of vendors greeting customers in low, careful tones.

They followed Sarah through the main thoroughfare until she stopped before a leaning inn lit with soft yellow light. A simple iron sign showed a mug of mead and a bed. Relief washed over James at the sight—shelter, warmth, a door with a lock.

"Looks like this will do," Sarah announced.

Inside, the tavern was bright but somber. The smell of wood smoke and warm food wrapped gently around them, though the subdued conversations seemed to fold in on themselves whenever a stranger passed.

Sarah approached the bar, set a gold coin down, and said, "Two rooms, please."

The innkeeper stared at her for a moment too long—Calculating? Confused? Suspicious?—before silently exchanging the coin for two bronze keys.

Sarah turned toward the stairs and handed one key to James. "I assumed you two wanted a room together," she said with a smirk.

"Shut up," James muttered, cheeks burning. Lusin's soft laugh didn't help. Sarah's cackle echoed up the stairwell.

The key turned easily in the old lock and the rough wood door swung open. The room smelled faintly musky but felt like paradise after the swamps—solid walls, dry floors, a bed that tilted slightly but held its shape. James dropped his pack, stripping off his damp cloak, sighing in relief. He left them where they fell and moved gratefully towards the bed. Until he realized he was alone.

He looked back for Lusin and found him lingering in the hall.

"Lusin? Is something wrong?"

The serpent prince blinked, then stepped inside and locked the door. "I thought I saw something."

"Anything I should worry about?"

"I'm not sure," Lusin admitted.

James waved it off as he began to remove his shirt—mostly because he was too tired to process anything else—then froze as he spotted the creeping black lines crawling up his arm. V-shaped marks climbed past his wrist almost to his elbow, darker than before. His pulse stumbled.

Lusin noticed.

James yanked his sleeve down. "No, it's nothing," he lied too quickly.

Silence dropped between them like a stone.

"So…" he tried, scratching his neck, "I'm exhausted. I think I'll just go to bed."

Lusin didn't move, watching him with that steady, unsettling quiet. James patted the bed beside him.

"Come on, Lusin. You look like you could use the rest too."

After a hesitant glance at the door, Lusin approached. The bed creaked under their combined weight. James immediately wrapped an arm around his shoulders, pulling him close. Lusin melted into the embrace, though a thin strand of tension remained coiled beneath his skin.

"Hey," James murmured, lifting Lusin's chin until their eyes met. "What's wrong?"

"I believe we are being followed," Lusin admitted. "I sensed someone in the swamps—and I had hoped they would lose our trail. But it seems they may not have."

James considered this, then managed a faint smile. "Well, no one would dare follow a basilisk into its lair, right?"

Lusin blinked uncertainly.

"Whatever or whoever it is," James said, brushing a thumb over Lusin's cheek, "we'll handle it in the morning."

Lusin softened, leaning into his touch. "Yes, my Sun," he whispered.

James's heart fluttered at the name. He leaned in. Lusin met him halfway. Their lips touched—cool and soft, fleeting and warm. When they parted, Lusin's fingers lingered against his cheek, reluctant to leave.

"Rest, James," he murmured. "I will keep watch."

James traced a final slow line along Lusin's cheek, savoring the moment, before letting his hand fall to the sheets. The faint sound of water lapping beneath the city scored the silence. Amber lamplight flickered against the fog outside, painting rippling gold along the walls.

For the first time in ages, James let his eyes close without fear.

Lusin's cool fingers drifted through his hair, steady and rhythmic.

But deep beneath the warmth of that moment, something stirred—a whisper of danger, unseen yet undeniably present.

Dorchas was not as still as it seemed.

CHAPTER 21
THE STRANGER

A rustle of cloth and the squeak of a floorboard woke Lusin.

For a single breath, confusion clouded his mind—thick and disorienting. He didn't remember falling asleep. He never fell asleep on duty, not when James was with him, not when danger lingered in the corners of every shadow in Dorchas. Yet exhaustion had caught him off guard, stealing precious moments of awareness. He could feel James's warmth pressed beside him, steady and familiar... and something else. Something cold. Something wrong. A presence that did not belong.

Instinct surged faster than conscious thought. In one fluid motion, he seized the long silver dagger beneath his pillow, rolled and struck toward the dark shape looming beside the bed. Green light flared along the dagger's edge, spraying golden sparks across the room in a brief, violent bloom that threw every surface into sharp relief.

The sight revealed by that light froze his blood.

A man—if he qualified as such—was hunched over James like a vulture poised above a carcass. His skin shimmered faintly green and gold in the magical glow, though Lusin couldn't tell if the colors were from the light or the man himself. His flesh was uneven and lumpy, as though someone had molded him by hand and then lost interest halfway through.

Wide, yellow, bloodshot eyes bulged from their sockets, ringed with square, sickly scales. Scruffy black brows met in a jagged tangle below greasy, unkempt hair. Where lips should have been, there was only a warped stretch of skin peeled back into a twisted smile full of chipped, yellow teeth.

The dagger's tip rested at the creature's throat—but Lusin couldn't finish the strike.

Because the intruder's long, knobby fingers—each tipped with a black claw—were wrapped firmly around James's neck.

"Hello, Lusin," the thing crooned, voice smooth and wrong. The sound made Lusin's stomach pitch. "Long have I wanted to speak with you."

The black claws drummed lazily against James's vulnerable skin, leaving faint red crescents. James lay limp, enchanted, his body unnaturally still. Too still. His chest barely rose and fell. Lusin's heart pounded so violently he felt each beat in his fingertips.

Rage didn't just rise—it detonated. A primal, possessive fury consumed him. No one laid filthy hands on his Sun and lived. Power surged behind his eyes, basilisk magic sharpening his vision, ready to strike, ready to kill this loathsome creature where it crouched. The intruder must have sensed the shift, because it hissed, mocking and gleeful.

"Now, now," he warned. "We wouldn't want any accidents."

The creature squeezed and James's body jerked. His blue eyes snapped open, dazed and glassy.

"Lusin…" he whispered, voice hoarse.

The single word shattered Lusin's concentration. The sight of those blue eyes—open, unfocused, vulnerable—forced him to slam his own shut. Pain burst behind his eyelids from the abrupt halt of his basilisk stare, but he refused to let it show.

When he opened them again, slow and careful, the fury was gone. In its place burned something colder, sharper, more lethal.

The creature only grinned wider.

"There we go. I knew we'd reach an understanding," it jeered, delighted.

"What do you want?" Lusin hissed, his snake fangs extending. "If you harm him, I swear—"

"I'm aware of that, love," the thing interrupted.

The endearment—the mockery of it—twisted Lusin's stomach in revulsion.

In the creature's left hand gleamed a short brass dagger. The sight of it made his pulse spike. The blade hovered dangerously near James's neck, drifting with casual threat. Lusin pressed his own dagger into the intruder's scaled throat, piercing his hide. Blood beaded along the blade, but the creature didn't so much as flinch.

Instead, he continued towards James's throat. Lusin hissed as he drove the dagger deeper but the creature didn't waver. It hooked the tip of the blade beneath the silver chain around James's neck and lifted the chain until the crystal compass tumbled out of his shirt into the weak light. The crystal swung in the sickly light, its glow faint... except for a tiny pulse of white deep within, like a heartbeat trapped in glass.

"I know what you're after," the creature said, voice bright with mockery. "A handy little toy, but unnecessary. I know where your prize lies."

Lusin didn't blink. "Where is the key?" he demanded, every syllable brittle with restrained violence.

"In the heart of the swamp," the intruder purred, "beyond the fields of poison gas. This one—" he jostled James's limp body, making Lusin's entire world tilt. "This one would never survive it. But you... you are sturdier than this soft little thing. You're like me."

Revulsion crawled like insects beneath Lusin's skin. The creature leaned closer, licking his chipped teeth with a forked tongue. The gesture made bile burn the back of Lusin's throat.

"Oh, I may not be pretty like you," he leered, "but you'll be surprised how alike we are."

Lusin tilted his dagger until the tip scraped against the creature's collarbone, forcing him back. More blood welled, dripping in thin streams, but the monster shivered as though savoring the pain.

Disgust deepened in Lusin's gut, but the claim—the knowledge of the key—kept his hand from ending this. If there was even a chance this thing spoke the truth, he couldn't risk it. Not when time was running far too quickly.

And then—the creature moved with lightning quickness.

The bronze blade flashed once, clean and cruel. The torn fabric of James's sleeve fell away to reveal the curse: the black lines creeping halfway toward James's elbow, the sigils pulsing faintly beneath the skin.

Lusin's breath caught.

When? How?

How long had James been hiding this from him?

Guilt and terror crashed together in his chest. The fever. The waiting. The sight of James motionless in that farmhouse bed. The helplessness of not being able to save him. Those memories resurfaced like drowning nightmares.

Time was slipping away.

He was losing James.

He couldn't waste another heartbeat.

The creature's voice slithered through his spiraling thoughts. "I can show you where it is. I can take you there."

Every part of Lusin's instinct screamed to kill him. End the threat. End the insult. Tear him apart for daring to touch James. But logic—cold, punishing logic—held his hand still.

"What do you want?" Lusin asked again, voice carved from stone.

The smile that spread across the creature's face was inhuman. "I want you, Lusin."

Lusin's grip tightened on his dagger. "And if I refuse?"

"Then I kill him."

The intruder's claws tightened. Blood beaded along James's throat. Lusin nearly lost control; it was only the faint rise and fall of James's chest, barely perceptible, that anchored him.

"And in exchange?" Lusin forced out.

"Come away with me," the monster rasped, trembling with excitement. "And I'll guide you to the key you seek."

Lusin twisted his dagger—bone cracked beneath the pressure. The creature shuddered, not with pain, but something far darker.

"I will go with you…" Lusin said, voice low and dangerous.

The beast's eyes lit up.

"…on one condition."

"Name it."

"James and Sarah are not to be harmed. In any way."

The smile faltered. The creature's eyes flashed with irritation, but Lusin did not wait for refusal—he drove controlled lightning through his blade, searing the wound. The creature jerked, then hissed.

"Done. Come," he rasped. "We go now."

Lusin rose slowly, refusing to turn his back. Every movement the creature made was met with the tip of Lusin's dagger tracking him. When the intruder stomped toward the door, leaving filthy footprints across the floorboards, Lusin allowed himself one moment—only one.

He knelt beside James.

He brushed trembling fingers through golden hair, memorizing every soft curve of his cheek, every breath.

He bent close and whispered, "I'm sorry, James. Please understand. I do this for you."

He pressed a soft kiss to James's lips—a promise, a plea, a farewell.

Then he conjured a tiny white serpent. It slid from his sleeve and coiled at James's heart, invisible beneath the blankets. A living tether. A line of safety. Constant reassurance.

He unfastened the crystal compass from James's neck and looped it around his own. It would keep him from being misled… and ensure that James couldn't follow.

Straightening, Lusin stepped toward the door. Each step tore him apart. James's heartbeat pulsed softly at the back of his mind through the serpent—a fragile lifeline he clung to like air.

Three days, he swore.

No more.

He followed the creature down the hall. As they passed Sarah's room, a second white serpent slipped from his cuff and wriggled beneath her door, carrying a single, urgent command: Protect him.

The creature didn't notice.

They stepped into the night. Dorchas's lamps glowed faintly through the fog, reflecting off the black water like dying stars. The creature led him to a secluded dock where a blackened, half-rotten boat waited—slimy, riddled with holes, as though it had crawled from the lake's depths to meet them.

The creature gestured grandly for him to board. Lusin stepped onto the swaying planks without hesitation, settling onto the ruined bench. The beast's stare crawled over him like oil. He ignored it.

As the oar dipped into the water, the boat began to glide into the darkness. Lusin turned back toward the faint outline of the city—toward James.

His Sun.

Every inch they drifted away tore a fresh wound through him. The crystal compass hung heavy around his neck with the weight of his betrayal.

He clutched the crystal at his throat and swore silently:

Three days, my Sun.

I will return to you.

CHAPTER 22
THE MISSING PRINCE

"**J**ames! You open this door right NOW!"

Sarah's voice rang in James's ears like a cracked bell, sharp and unrelenting. The pounding of her fist rattled through the wood and sent a spike of pain through his skull. He jolted upright, chest heaving, heart racing from being dragged so violently out of sleep. For a moment he didn't even remember where he was. His breath fogged in the cold air of the little room, and his limbs trembled with the abrupt wakefulness.

He scrubbed at his eyes, groaning as he pushed himself upright. His body felt heavy and sluggish, as though sleep still clung to him like a wet blanket. The knocking continued—furious, explosive.

After a groggy stretch, he stumbled toward the door, each step wobbling. "What's her problem?" he muttered toward Lusin without thinking. His sleep-fogged fingers fumbled the lock several times before it finally clicked. He swung the door open mid-yawn.

Sarah filled the frame like a storm cloud, jaw clenched, eyes wild.

"What is it?" James asked, yawning so wide it nearly cracked his jaw.

"Where's Lusin?" she demanded.

The question sliced through his fatigue like a blade. "What do you mean 'where's Lusin'? He's right—" He turned to point at the bed.

Silence.

An empty mattress.

The sight didn't register at first—his mind refused to process it. The bed's musky sheets, the dent where Lusin had slept, the faint imprint of where a body had been... but no Lusin.

"Lusin?" James called weakly. He scanned the small room like the basilisk might have shrunk himself to hide beneath the single wooden chair or behind the threadbare quilt. His stomach tightened. Maybe Lusin had gone downstairs for water? For food?

He shoved past Sarah, panic cutting through the last threads of sleep, and half ran, half fell down the hall. Sarah called something behind him, but he ignored it. He took the rickety stairs two at a time, breath tearing at his throat, and jumped the last four.

"Lusin?!" he shouted into the tavern, voice cracking.

Every conversation froze mid-sentence. Heads turned. A few cloaked figures stiffened. The creak of a chair echoed too loudly. James didn't care. He hunted the room for the sliver of gold he loved—those inhuman, beautiful eyes—anywhere. Nowhere.

A hand clamped his shoulder and he yelped. Sarah yanked him backward, dragging him up the stairs with embarrassing ease. She shoved him into the hallway and pinned him to the wall before slapping a hand over his mouth.

"Will you shut up!" she hissed. Her breath was hot on his cheek, her grip iron. "Lusin's gone! I wanted to know if you knew why he left—or where."

Only the first two words landed.

Lusin's gone.

The words collapsed into his chest like a stone. His lungs seized. The hall seemed to compress around him, the dim lanternlight flickering too harshly. Lusin wouldn't leave—not like this, not without waking him, not without saying a word.

He tore Sarah's hand away.

"How do you know he's gone?! He would *never* leave me like this!" he snapped, the words spilling out hot, raw, too fast. Anger surged to fill the bottomless pit forming in his chest.

Sarah flinched at the force of his voice, then steadied herself, pity softening her expression—an expression that made everything hurt worse.

"He… he left this with me. It gave me a message," she said quietly.

From behind her shoulder, a small, pure white snake lifted its head. Its tongue flicked gently at the air, golden eyes shining with a painfully familiar warmth.

James's heart cracked.

"I assumed he left one for you too," Sarah added.

A prickle ran up James's right arm—like static, like something alive moving beneath his skin. Panic flared. He jerked his sleeve up to shake it off—only to freeze.

His sleeve was neatly cut to the elbow.

The curse marks—dark, branching sigils—exposed.

It hadn't been like that last night.

From the torn cloth, an identical white serpent slid gracefully into the open, gliding up his arm. It curled along his shoulder, nuzzled his jaw with delicate familiarity, then coiled near his left ear like a guardian spirit.

"James…" Lusin's voice whispered, soft as breath.

James's knees nearly gave way.

"Lusin?" he croaked. Hope surged violently through him, burning off the chill that had been creeping in.

"James… I'm sorry. Please understand… I do this… for you."

The whispered cadence wrapped around his heart. James's grip on the railing tightened so hard his fingers went numb.

"But why, Lusin? What are you doing? Where did you go?" he begged, voice cracking.

The message repeated. No change. No answers.

Just a loop—Lusin's voice trapped in a sliver of magic.

The message wasn't a conversation. It was a goodbye.

The hall tilted. James swallowed hard, trying to breathe through the pressure crushing his chest.

"What did it say?" Sarah asked softly.

"He said… he's sorry. That he did this… for me," James whispered, the words scraping out of him.

This is a nightmare. Any second he'll walk up behind me. Any second—

"Did it say what he was doing?" she pressed.

James shook his head. Thoughts battered him from every angle—

Did I misread everything?

Is he angry with me?

Did I do something wrong?

Wasn't I enough?

Nothing stayed long enough to answer.

"Was he acting strangely last night?" Sarah asked.

"What's *THAT* supposed to mean?!" James exploded, raw and frayed.

Sarah jerked back, then forced her voice calm. "I mean—did he do anything to suggest he might take off?!"

James's mind scrambled through memories. "He was tense. He said he thought we were being followed."

Sarah nodded slowly, absorbing it. "We should—"

"We have to go after him," James cut her off. "Wherever he's gone, he can't be alone."

Sarah dropped her hands, crossing her arms tightly. Her white snake climbed to her shoulder, settling there like a sentinel.

"What? You think we shouldn't?!" he roared.

He hated how easily she distrusted Lusin. He'd thought she'd changed. After the Wastes… after Grandma's farm… after they *tag-teamed* nannying him… he'd thought she had grown to believe in Lusin.

"I told you to keep your voice down, idiot," she muttered, exasperated. "He left me a message too, *remember*? He asked me to look after you until he returns. I think it's safe to assume he intends to come back. We can wait here."

"He said he's coming back?" The words softened his fury, hope igniting again.

"He told me to watch you until he *returns*." She shrugged. "So—yes. He plans to."

Relief washed over him. Thin, fragile—but real.

Still—

"But why would he leave me behind?"

"Because he thinks it's too dangerous—or because your curse has spread, again." She nodded toward his arm. He tugged at the torn sleeve, but it still revealed everything.

"Really, how long were you planning to hide that?" Sarah said. "He worries more about you than anyone."

"That's *why* I hid it," James snapped. "He's stressed enough. And it hasn't spread *that* far—" He stopped. Even to his own ears, the excuse was a joke. "We still have time," he muttered, uncertain.

Sarah's expression shifted sharply. "James—besides Lusin, was anything else missing?"

"I don't know, Sarah, I was busy looking for *Lusin*," he snapped, frustrated and hurting.

"You *idiot*," she hissed. "The key and the necklace. Do you still have them?"

James shoved his hand into his pocket—fingers brushing cool metal. He pulled out the air key. The pearl glowed faintly.

"Good. Put it away," she whispered, shielding it. "And the necklace?"

His fingers went to his neck, intending to hook the chain with his thumb.

Nothing.

His pulse spiked. He patted frantically. Empty.

"I don't have the crystal," he breathed.

They tore back up the stairs. In under a minute, they overturned the room—blankets, floorboards, bags, the chair, even the space beneath the mattress.

Nothing.

"Well, that confirms it," Sarah said, hands planted on her hips. "He took the necklace, but not the map or the key. And your sleeve wasn't like that when you went to bed, right?"

"Yeah, yeah," James muttered, half to himself. "We know."

"Then obviously he saw the curse spreading and went after the key himself."

"Why would he do that?" The question ripped out of him like a wound.

"Because he's trying to protect you! Idiot!" Sarah yelled. She turned and threw her hands in the air, emphasising her frustration.

James braced both hands on the rickety chair, head bowed. His breath shook. "So we just sit and wait? Sarah, you remember the last guardian—we barely survived *together*. If it weren't for—whatever the FUCK this is—" He shook his cursed arm. "—we wouldn't have."

His voice cracked upward. He didn't care who heard.

"And we're supposed to believe Lusin can face the next one alone? YOU can wait if you want. I'm going after him. I'm going to get him back, and nothing is going to stand in my way!"

He snatched up his pack and stormed out. Sarah cursed under her breath and sprinted after him.

"James! Wait! We don't even know where he's gone!"

"We have the map! If we hurry, that will get us close enough!"

"Damn it!" She bolted into her room, grabbed her gear, and ran.

He thundered down the stairs into the tavern. Heads turned. He ignored them. He shoved past the doors and burst into Dorchas's night—eternal, swirling black above a maze of lamps and walkways.

No sunrise.

No stars.

Just endless night.

No time to think about it.

He scanned the streets, then marched in a direction that felt like it could eventually lead to a dock—left, then right, then right again, planks groaning under his boots. Lamps flickered. Ropes creaked. Dorchas breathed like an old, tired ship.

Finally—a dock.

A long, crooked pier stretched over the water like a reaching arm. Nets hung like shadows. Huts hunched against railings. Halfway down, a set of stairs dropped to a lower platform.

James descended fast. An old fisherman in oilskins was hauling a crate from deck to dock. James skidded to a halt.

"You there! How much to rent your boat?" he barked.

The man glanced up—and froze. His jaw dropped. The crate slipped from his hands.

"Hey! I asked you how much to rent your boat!" James snapped.

A heavy thump hit him—Sarah landing against his back. She yanked his hood down hard over his hair.

"James, you moron. Keep your damn head covered," she hissed. Then, to the fisherman, switching instantly to polite efficiency: "Yes. We want to hire a boat into the swamps and buy whatever gear we'll need."

The old man blinked several times, then nodded gravely. He jerked his chin toward the boat.

"Aye," he rasped. "Climb aboard."

CHAPTER 23
GIVING CHASE

James sat at the bow of the boat, his posture rigid and his eyes fixed on the horizon. The wooden seat beneath him vibrated faintly with each churn of the small engine, but he barely felt it. The vessel glided through the black water in a steady, hypnotic rhythm—far too slow for what his heart demanded.

To an outside observer, he might have seemed calm—composed, even—but the faint tension in his shoulders betrayed him. His jaw flexed every few seconds. His fingers twitched restlessly against his knee. Inside, his thoughts collided like waves in a storm.

He hated sitting still.

Stillness meant thinking.

Thinking meant feeling.

And feeling… meant losing control.

Acting—any kind of motion—was easier. Movement dulled the ache. Focusing on a target, a task, a physical goal—anything—kept the emotions at bay long enough to breathe. Yet now, there was nothing left to do but sit and wait. The low hum of the engine and the soft churn of the water were his only distractions, and even those did little to quiet the turmoil inside him. His mind circled the same painful truths:

Lusin gone, taken by something terrible, and he hadn't been awake to stop it.

The little white snake lay curled contentedly in his lap, its body warm against the chill of the swamp air. It tucked its small head into his palm and leaned into his thumb as he absently stroked the delicate ridge above its eye. He felt its tiny heartbeat against his skin—a steady pulse, mirroring Lusin's from miles away. The tiny creature had become his anchor, holding him together every time panic tried to tear him apart.

He had lost count of how many times he'd replayed Lusin's message. He wasn't searching for hidden meaning anymore. He had listened to the same fractured apology again and again—not because it helped, but because it was the only connection left to the basilisk's voice. That calm, steady voice that had always made the world feel less chaotic.

He could feel Sarah's gaze burning into the back of his head. She had been watching him for hours—quiet but restless, shifting her weight, rubbing her arms for warmth, drumming her fingers on her thigh as if waiting for him to break. He wished she would stop—just find something, any-thing, else to do. Her concern was obvious and well-meaning, but it only deepened the hollow ache inside him. Nothing she could say or do would make him okay. He would only be whole when he had Lusin back.

Even the old fisherman's eyes joined hers from time to time. He wasn't as blatant, but James still felt the weight of the man's curiosity whenever it landed on him—like a pebble dropped into a lake, creating ripples that refused to settle. The captain had barely spoken since Sarah negotiated their passage and purchased supplies. Even now, the silence between them carried a strange, uneasy energy—one that made James's skin crawl. Every few minutes the man would glance up from his wheel, studying James with a sort of careful fascination.

Then it clicked.

The old man had recognized him.

Damn it.

James's stomach twisted. In his determination to chase after Lusin, he'd forgotten to keep his head covered. Sarah was right—again. Subtlety had never been his strength. He grimaced at the thought of the old captain gossiping about the "missing prince" once they were gone. The image of gossip spreading like wildfire through Dorchas made his pulse spike. He could practically hear the whispers already.

There was nothing he could do about it now. Threatening him or offering gold would only make him more suspicious. For now, all James could do was pretend not to notice and pray the old man kept his mouth shut.

Gradually, the deep black sky shifted to steel gray, then to the color of milk. The pale fog thickened around them, rolling back in lazy, sluggish waves as they neared the edge of the black swamp. A cold breeze ghosted across James's face, carrying the scent of stagnant water and something sour he refused to name.

This part of the Delta Swamps looked... wrong.

The trees here were fewer and black as charcoal, stripped bare in jagged patches as if something had scraped their bark clean. Wisps of gray moss hung from their branches like ghostly fingers reaching for the water below. The water itself remained dark, but now ribbons of an acid-green sheen rippled across its surface, shifting like oil caught in weak light.

Every breath tasted of rot and salt.

Every sound seemed swallowed by the fog.

The air pressed heavily against their lungs, a damp weight that stuck to skin and hair. Mist crawled in slow folds across the water, and the sunlight filtering through felt thin and uncertain—more like a memory of light than light itself.

The boat cut through the green film with a wet hiss. For a long time, the only sounds were the slosh of water against the hull and the hum of the motor. James focused on them like lifelines.

Then, a sudden hiss and guttural growl shattered the fragile peace.

James's head snapped toward the sound. A massive alligator, its scales like polished armor plates, was resting itself on a rotten log. It opened its jaws in warning, flashing rows of ancient teeth. Its exhale fogged the air as it slid into the swamp with a violent splash.

James's breath hitched. He'd never seen one before—at least not alive. The raw power in that single motion made him instinctively clutch the little white snake against his chest, shielding it with his arm. Rationally, he knew the creature posed no threat to them on the boat. But his body refused to relax. He'd already lost Lusin. He couldn't bear to lose this last piece of him, too.

Then the hum of the engine sputtered. Once. Twice. Then died completely. The boat drifted, swaying gently in the water.

James straightened, frowning. Sarah's expression tightened. The fisherman simply stared ahead with grim resignation.

He tucked the little snake safely into his shirt and stalked toward the wheelhouse.

"This is as far as I go," the old fisherman announced flatly.

James blinked. They were still at least a full day from where the map indicated the next key lay.

"Please, sir," Sarah said, her tone polite but strained. "Will you at least take us to shore?"

"I cannot take you any further," the man repeated, sneering.

James felt irritation coil tight in his chest, wrapping around his ribs like a vise. Every wasted second stretched the distance between him and Lusin. He took a step forward, but Sarah's arm shot out across his chest, stopping him.

"Then we'll buy your lifeboat," she said, pointing to one of the two dinghies lashed to the deck. "Give us a moment to load it, and we'll be on our way."

"Hold on now, little missy," the man leered, stroking his beard. "Didn't say I was gonna sell it."

Sarah's eyes narrowed. "We're prepared to make a generous offer."

James's patience snapped.

Hard.

Every second lost was a knife turning deeper. The man's smugness grated across every raw nerve he had left. Sarah pressed a hand to his chest again—her silent plea for restraint—but James's glare made it clear restraint was rapidly dying.

The old man smirked. "I doubt any offer you've got will match a prince's ransom."

The words hit like a slap. So, he hadn't intended to be amicable after all.

Before the man could even blink, Sarah dropped her arm—as if granting permission, not that he needed it—and James moved.

In a blur of motion he sidestepped Sarah, drew his knife, and struck. The fisherman's knife flew from his hand, spinning high into the air before splashing uselessly into the swamp. James seized the man by his coat, hauled him off his feet, and slammed him against the wheelhouse wall so hard the whole boat shuddered.

"Listen up, old man," James snarled, face inches from the captain's. His voice was low, lethal. "You had your chance to earn a little gold and live your miserable little life in peace. But you crossed the wrong line. Now we're taking your boat, your supplies, and if you're lucky, we won't tie you to the helm and burn you with the ship."

The man's face drained of color. His eyes darted desperately to Sarah, who now stood beside James—her expression calm but her eyes glowing like embers. She lifted her hand, and fire blossomed between her fingers.

"No! Please! Mercy!" the man squeaked, voice cracking. "I beg you, Prince James!"

Pathetic.

"Fine," James said coldly, lowering him slightly without releasing him. The man sagged in relief.

Then James turned and hurled him overboard.

Sarah gave him a look somewhere between disapproval and amusement. He returned it with defiance—then finally sighed.

"Fine," he muttered, slicing through the ropes that held the spare lifeboat. The dinghy fell into the water with a splash.

"But I'm still burning the ship," James added darkly.

"I expected no less," Sarah said with a crooked smile, already helping him load supplies.

Smoke curled into the sky behind them, thick and oily. James didn't look back. His blood was still hot and his pulse refused to slow. The smaller boat rocked gently beneath them as Sarah rowed in silence, giving him the solitude she knew he needed.

They had considered keeping the larger vessel—the motor would have been useful—but it was too noisy, too heavy, too obvious. The lifeboat was faster, quieter, easier to hide. The shore wasn't far now; the burning ship behind them was a message to anyone who thought to follow.

James sat at the bow again, eyes fixed forward. The little snake peeked from his shirt and nuzzled at the curve of his jaw, seeking reassurance. He smiled faintly and tucked it back into the safety of his collar.

"Maybe we should have killed him," Sarah said after a long silence.

James tilted his head slightly toward her. "That's not like you," he said cautiously.

"It's bad that he recognized you," she said grimly. "If he makes it back to Dorchas, the whole kingdom will know the Prince of Valenor was there."

"So?" James muttered. What did it matter if they knew? By the time word reached Solis, he'd already have Lusin back—or be dead trying.

"*So*," Sarah sighed sharply, "there'll be hunters, James. Soldiers. Assassins. You might be ready to fight, but traveling with half the kingdom on our trail will make it harder for both of us."

He shrugged. "Let them come."

His tone was flat, but bitterness clung to it. Maybe a fight would be good. At least a fight was something he could punch, stab, or burn. At least it was something he could control.

"Even you can't be that reckless," Sarah muttered. "You practically stormed across the entire city without your hood. It's a miracle we made it out."

James didn't argue. She was right—again. She usually was. But he didn't care. None of it mattered next to the singular purpose beating inside him like a second heartbeat.

He thought of the night he first met Lusin—the bandits, the chaos, the shock of golden eyes in the dark. No one had dared threaten him when Lusin was near. His presence alone had made the world feel safer.

Now, without him, everything felt wrong.

He didn't care if people came after them.

He didn't care about danger, the kingdom, or the consequences.

The only thing that mattered was finding Lusin—his partner, his protector, his other half.

He tightened his grip on the boat's edge and stared into the pale, rotting horizon.

No matter what it took, he would bring Lusin back.

CHAPTER 24
THE WATER KEY

Lusin despised the beast.

He spent every waking moment imagining the ways he could kill it—slowly, beautifully, painfully. These dark thoughts were his only comfort, the only thing that dulled the sharp ache that gnawed at his heart. This monster was the reason he'd been forced to abandon James. Even if that hadn't been true, Lusin would have destroyed it on principle alone.

Every time the creature breathed, its scraping, bubbling exhale made Lusin's skin tighten with revulsion. The sound seemed to vibrate in the air—wet and rattling—like something dead trying to mimic the breathing of living things. Even from several paces away, the smell of it lingered: metallic, rotten, tinged faintly with sulfur.

They had crossed the lake in silence that first morning, the only sound the beast's rasping, labored breath. The boat rocked under their weight, the hull creaking with every shift of water. Lusin never took his eyes off the monster. He was certain it had a name, but he had no interest in knowing it. To him, it was nothing more than a feral animal—unworthy of a name, unworthy of thought.

By afternoon, the decomposing boat scraped against the far shore. The vessel groaned as if relieved to be free of the monster's weight, then sank into the muck as if allowed to die now that its duty was fulfilled.

The land beyond was soft and dark, black mud streaked with sickly green grass that clumped together in uneven tufts. Even walking across it felt wrong; the earth gave beneath Lusin's boots as if it were breathing slowly.

As they trudged forward, the trees thinned, and the swamp opened into a wide grassy flat where the ground quivered underfoot. The sky draped low overhead, heavy with mist that clung to Lusin's hair and settled cold on his skin. Here, they made their first camp.

Lusin did not sleep. He refused to let his guard down while in the creature's presence. He sat with his back to a rock, daggers resting across his knees, watching the beast's warped silhouette by the faint, ghostly glow of distant swamp fireflies.

Yet despite his determination, the next thing he remembered was waking in the faint gray before dawn—eyes stinging, lungs burning—and finding the beast lying beside him, grinning wide enough to split its scaly face.

Instinct took over. Lusin slashed and stabbed, his claws slicing through flesh and muscle, but at the last instant he stopped short of a killing blow. He still needed the beast alive—for James.

Black-green tinged scarlet blood spattered his arm, hissing faintly as it hit the damp earth. But the creature didn't even flinch. It smiled wider, teeth slick with its own blood.

Lusin's pulse thudded in his ears. This was the second time he'd fallen asleep without realizing it. He didn't need rest the way other races did—food and calm were usually enough to sustain him for days. Even under the crushing worry he'd felt waiting for James to wake in Grandma's farmhouse, he'd gone four days without sleep.

Yet here, he'd blacked out twice in as many nights.

His jaw clenched. He was certain the creature was responsible. Something about its presence, its aura, the sickly smell it exuded—something dragged him into unconsciousness without warning. It was deliberate. Mocking.

Still, the beast seemed to be leading him in the right direction. The faint light within the crystal compass glowed stronger with every mile. That, and the steady rhythm of James's heartbeat echoing faintly at the back of his mind, were the only things that kept him from tearing the monster apart.

By afternoon the ground began to firm beneath his boots. The grass rose to his waist, green shoots with tan tops, thick and endless. The air turned sour—at first a faint whiff of rotten eggs, then an overwhelming stench that burned his throat and eyes. His vision watered. Even for a basilisk, the sting was intense.

Just when he thought he could take no more, the smell vanished completely.

That sudden absence terrified him.

"Oh, it's still there, love," the beast crooned, amused. "That's the nature of the Poison Flats. The gas deadens your senses before it kills you. Normal creatures choke on it. Lucky for us—we're not normal, are we?"

Its voice crawled down his spine like insects. It took another few steps, chuckling, and added, "Careful with your lightning, pretty thing. One spark, and this whole field will go up like tinder."

The way it said *pretty thing* made his skin crawl. The claws tapping the grass as it walked sounded like bone scraping bone.

By nightfall, Lusin's restraint was wearing thin. The creature had taken to touching his hair whenever it pleased, claws snagging in his silvery-blue strands as it murmured nonsense. Each time, Lusin answered with a new cut, a new bruise—but it never learned. If anything, it seemed to enjoy the pain. The more he hurt it, the more affectionate it became.

The second night pushed him beyond his limits. He sat awake for hours, glaring into the darkness, forcing his body to stay alert. He repeated James's heartbeat to himself like a mantra. He tried to keep his breathing steady, his eyes open—

Yet somehow, he drifted off again without realizing—and woke to the creature beside him once more, claws stroking his hair like a lover's touch.

Something inside him broke.

His roar split the dawn. He struck without hesitation or mercy, tearing into the creature with claws and fury, shredding flesh, snapping bone. His lightning surged through every strike, its sparks deadened by the wet gush of blood. Hot gore sprayed across his arms and face. He didn't care. Each strike was a release, a promise that this torment would end here.

There were cleaner ways to kill it, but he didn't want clean. He wanted to feel it die.

He raked his claws down the creature's chest and prepared to tear its throat out. But his final blow cut through nothing but air. The monster was gone.

A grotesque gurgling rose behind him. Lusin spun, eyes glowing red, and saw the beast thirty feet away, standing amid the blood-soaked grass. Its mangled body quivered; bones jutted through shredded skin. The thing was barely holding itself together.

Then—it laughed.

The laugh began as a wet wheeze and swelled into shrieking hilarity that echoed across the flats.

"That's the way, love!" it wheezed. "You sure are a spirited one!"

Lusin could only stare. He had mutilated it beyond recognition—ripped it open until half its body hung in ribbons and its entrails littered the grass in piles—yet it still laughed. Blood poured freely from its wounds, pooling at its feet.

"It's all right, Lusin. There's no harm in a little fun."

His stomach turned.

The beast wiped blood from its mouth and turned away, shambling southward as if nothing had happened. When Lusin didn't follow, it twisted its head backward—completely backward—with a sickening snap.

"The key isn't far now."

He followed, silent and seething. As they walked, he watched in revulsion as its wounds began to close. The skin bubbled like hot wax, edges stretching and knitting together. Bones slid back beneath reforming flesh. The gore dried and cracked away until the creature's hyde gleamed slick and whole again.

Next time, he vowed, he would take its head.

Hours passed. The crystal shone brighter with each step, pulsing like a heartbeat. The sound of James's real heartbeat echoed faintly through the bond, soothing him, reminding him of why he endured this nightmare.

The flatlands began to shift again—grass thickening, boulders rising like ancient teeth from the earth. The breeze whispered faintly through the tall blades. Everything else was dead silent.

By midday, granite stones towered above him, polished and silver-gray under the pale sun. The monster slipped between a cluster of massive rocks and vanished. Lusin followed, daggers drawn. The compass glowed now like a tiny sun suspended from his neck.

He moved through the narrow passage, silent as breath, and emerged into a small clearing. The stones formed a natural wall around a circular patch of tall grass. In its center stood a small altar of polished granite, almost hidden in the green. High above, soft white clouds drifted across a gentle blue sky.

The creature stood before the altar, back to him, motionless. Lusin crept closer, blades ready. When the beast finally moved, it was to place a single clawed hand upon the altar's surface.

A burst of white light split the stone. The halves slid apart with a grinding sigh. The creature reached into the hollow and withdrew something that flashed blue and bronze in the sunlight.

It turned, smiling wider than ever. Its eyes gleamed—now unmistakably red—and it extended its hand toward Lusin.

In its palm rested a key: bronze filigree wrapped around a sapphire core, a short shaft with teeth on both sides. A twin to the air key from the Wastes.

But something was wrong.

The compass still blazed on its chain—the seal unbroken.

The guardian wasn't dead.

A cold dread slid down his spine.

He tried to raise his daggers, but his body refused to move. His limbs locked in place as if frozen solid.

The creature chuckled. "What's wrong, love?" it purred, stepping closer, holding the key inches from Lusin's face. "Isn't this what you came for? Take it."

Rage burned through him. He wanted to strike, to unleash his stare, his lightning—anything—but the spell held firm.

The key flickered and melted into the monster's flesh. Pale blue light crawled through the guardian's grotesque body until it settled in its chest. There the light grew and pulsed like a cold heartbeat.

The guardian came closer still, close enough for its rancid breath to fan over Lusin's cheek. One clawed hand lifted to trace the edge of his jaw, then his cheek, brushing the fine scales there. Lusin wanted to recoil, but he couldn't move.

No one was allowed to touch him like this.

No one but James.

"You are beautiful, Lusin," the guardian hissed, its forked tongue flicking against his cheek. "You belong with me. Not with that half-breed. He's being consumed by the curse—you know he doesn't have long. Stay with me, my love. We're the same. Monsters, you and I."

No.

He wasn't like this thing.

He was a basilisk, yes—but James had seen him as more. James had trusted him. Loved him. Lusin's heart surged with that memory, burning through the poison of the beast's words. Light erupted around him—acid green and radiant—as he fought to break free.

The spell began to weaken. His hands trembled as they began to inch forward.

Then—silence.

A hole opened inside his mind where James's heartbeat had rested.

The bond was gone. The effect of the loss of his Sun was instant. A deep, endless void yawned inside him and the cold of ice pumped through his veins.

The guardian's spell shattered and Lusin's back arched in response to the sudden chill and stillness. His daggers fell into the grass. Both hands flew to his head as if he could claw the emptiness away.

No... no, please no!

He desperately reached inward, searching for the familiar pulse—for his link to Sarah—for anything.

Nothing answered.

But, that wasn't possible. He had left the familiars with the express command to sit on James and Sarah's hearts, sending proof that they were alive to him at all times. He had not ended the spell. The only way the link could be severed is if the snakes were destroyed and the only way that could happen was if...

He staggered, then collapsed to his knees, trembling violently. His chest felt as though it were splitting open from the inside.

"James..." he whispered, the name breaking in his throat. "*No.*"

"What's the matter? Did you lose something *precious*, love?" The guardian's mocking tone sliced through the silence.

Lusin looked up, eyes wide with shock and fury. The creature was smiling, radiant with cruel delight.

He understood now.

It knew what had happened to James.

It had done this.

Somehow, it had taken everything from him.

The agony in his chest ignited into something blinding as his grief and rage found a target. His aura flared to life, green light searing through the haze until it blazed white-hot. His eyes bled red as his form began to shift, bones cracking, body stretching.

The guardian's grin widened in awe.

"That's it, Lusin!" it cried. "Show me the monster you truly are!"

CHAPTER 25
TRAP

James pushed across the grassy flats as fast as he dared without breaking into a full run. The protective mask over his mouth and nose made every breath feel shallow; the scratched goggles turned the world into a smeared, wavering pane of glass. He stumbled more than once but pressed on.

The last two nights had been miserable. The first had been as buggy and wet as their earliest, worst night in the swamps—but this time he didn't have Lusin's quiet presence to anchor him. He hadn't slept a wink. The second night, farther inland, was less infested but just as bleak and lonely.

If he shed tears in the dark, Sarah was kind enough to pretend she didn't hear.

Only sheer exhaustion finally dragged him under in the early hours. At dawn he felt heavier than ever—aching, hollow, dark bags under his eyes. His movements were mechanical, willpower moving him where strength could not.

As morning wore on, the air shifted from heavy green wetland to the faint taint of sulfur—rotten eggs at the edge of perception—until James's temples pulsed and his eyes burned. Sarah rummaged in one of the stubbornly heavy bags she'd refused to leave behind and pressed a mask and lenses into his hands with a curt order: *on, now*. He didn't argue.

The map said they were nearing the water key's general location. They had seen no sign of Lusin.

Around mid-morning, motion snagged James's eye: a knot of big, rag-black ravens gathered in the flats. Scavengers weren't unusual—but they were the first living things he'd seen since the sea of grass began. Before he understood why, his legs were already moving. He broke into a run, dread and need hot in his chest. Sarah called after him, then gave up and followed.

The ravens scattered. The scene beneath them was grisly. Tall grass lay flattened into wide swaths, and what remained stood painted dark with blood. Pools glistened; spatter arced in every direction; ragged lumps of flesh matted the earth. A couple of bolder birds clung to the largest pieces, ripping meat free with red slicked beaks.

"What happened here...?" Sarah breathed—airily, and also like she already knew.

It was recent. The pools were only half dried; the flesh still wet. A breeze sent ripples through the grass, and something else fluttered at the margin—torn leather on the lip of a blood pool. James stepped toward it—and froze. Tangled in another tuft, half soaked in bright red, a strip of black cloth with gold trim snapped in the wind.

A piece of Lusin's sleeve.

He freed the scrap with shaking fingers. Sarah leaned over his shoulder and gasped; she recognized the fabric too.

"Lusin was here," she said flatly.

"He was attacked," James managed, anger and fear roughening his voice. A narrow red trail led south. "He's hurt. We have to hurry!"

"James—wait!" She grabbed his shoulder and dug in. "Will you stop and think for once?" She gestured wide, sending another raven flapping. "Look. Really look. That's the only scrap of Lusin's clothes—but there are shreds of leather *everywhere*."

He looked. She was right: leather tatters scattered amid the gore, but not more pieces of Lusin's distinctive black and gold. His brain skidded in panic.

"What's your point?"

"My point is—it's clear Lusin was *doing* the attacking!" Even through the gear her fury carried.

"What does that matter? If he did this, he had a reason!" He didn't know why he was shouting—only that everything inside him hurt. Sarah gave him a knowing, maddening look.

"Where's the body…?" she asked a beat later.

"What?"

"If someone was torn apart like this, they would not survive. But there's no body."

"They must have—because they left a trail." He jabbed toward the crushed path running south.

"Something's not—"

"I don't care, Sarah!" he snapped through the mask. "Lusin was here, and it wasn't long ago. Whatever happened, it'll make sense once we find him."

He followed the trail. Sarah arched as she swore colorfully at the sky, then fell in at his heels.

They moved in tense silence. The blood thinned from a steady stream to a smear to occasional drops—then vanished. The path continued as clean, flattened grass, a purposeful line south.

By midday, silver-gray boulders dotted the flats like sleeping beasts. James slowed. The air was too still. The trail felt *too* clear. He gripped his blades and eased his steps. They were close—he could feel it—and something was very wrong.

The earth buckled.

A brownish-orange surge erupted from the torn ground and lunged for him—a living avalanche of snakes, thousands upon thousands.

"Sarah!" he shouted, as the writhing mass lashed around him. He slashed in wide arcs, shedding coils by the handful, but more poured forward to replace them. Teeth like needles pricked through cloth; rough scales rasped his skin.

His shirt shredded, the fabric tore away—and with it, Lusin's tiny white snake. Panic slammed through him.

He fought his way inward, frantic. A pinprick flash of white—there. In the center of the knot, his small companion writhed, tangled in torn fabric while heavier snakes bit and pulled from every angle.

"No!" James redoubled his effort, carving toward that little flake of snow—when hands seized his shoulders and hurled him back. He tumbled hard, hip and ribs jarring, blades clashing and sparking as they hit. The sparks flared—then blossomed into sudden fire, singeing his hair.

Realization hit him like a second impact.

"Sarah—*NO!*"

He looked up helplessly into slow motion. Sarah stood tall, hands raised before her masked face—summoning. Snakes latched onto her legs and arms, razoring at cloth and skin. Between her palms, a bead of fire snapped to life, then roared as the gas around them ignited.

Red fire swallowed everything.

The shockwave stole his hearing and left his vision pocked with stars. He lay stunned, then clawed back toward awareness. When the world steadied, he struggled upright. The blast had scoured a circle at least a hundred yards wide, grass charred to ash along with the seething nest. He suspected it was the steady coastal breeze that had kept the entire flat from going up.

Islands of flame burned on, fed by gas seeping from the black soil. He limped through the ruin, palm bracing his singed left arm, ears ringing so hard he couldn't tell if he was breathing. He passed what was left of his tiny snake—nothing but a blackened thread among other small corpses—and swallowed the pain down. He kept moving.

He found Sarah twenty feet from where she'd cast, sprawled on her back. Her hair and clothes were scorched; soot painted her skin. Miraculously, her mask and goggles were still in place.

"Sarah!" He dropped to his knees and checked her for injuries. Burns, yes—but nothing catastrophic. The fire in her blood must have shielded her from the worst of the blast.

"Hey. Sarah—wake up." He tapped her cheek with his fingertips. Nothing. He shook her shoulders gently. Her own little white snake slid out of her tunic and fell limp to the ashes. The sight stabbed him—but he stayed focused. "Come on. Wake up."

Her head lolled to the side. Blood trickled from her ear.

Panic clawed his chest. He ripped off her goggles; dazed eyes glimmered half-open beneath. He reached for her mask, hesitated—the little fires still burned, and the gas would only build if they snuffed them out. He made the command decision to remove the mask. He leaned close to listen—but his hearing was too blown to tell.

Tears spilled hot and unbidden. He couldn't breathe. He dragged off his suffocating mask and goggles and pulled her into his arms.

"Please, Sarah. Please don't die." He rocked her, his sister, and babbled apologies into the smoky haze. "I'm sorry. It's my fault. I'll listen from now on, I swear—just wake up. Please." Her body hung limp in his arms, deaf to his pleas.

He screamed a raw and ragged curse to the sky. He'd dragged her into this; he'd lost Lusin; he'd gotten himself cursed. Every terrible turn pointed back at him. He screamed until his throat was raw and his lungs ached. His tears fell freely, dotting Sarah's face.

Her body lurched. She gasped, sucking in life like a drowning swimmer breaking the surface.

"*Sarah?*" He held her steady as she clutched at her chest and belly. She coughed—wheezed—then found a rhythm.

"M—mask…" she rasped. He laughed through a sob, the relief flooding him making him giddy, and handed it over. She punched him weakly in the shoulder before slipping the gear back on, and he barked a brighter, shaken laugh as he tugged his own mask and lenses into place.

"I fail to see what's funny," she grumped, scrambling out of his arms and trying—and failing—to stand.

"Are you sure you're okay?" he asked, rising to brace her elbow and upper arm. She gave him a look. He remained unconvinced.

"I'm fine, James." She took another step—firmer this time.

"Well, you're bleeding," he said, pointing to his own ears. She touched beneath one strap, inspected her red fingers, and grimaced.

"I've got a headache, but I can still hear, so I'll live." She wiped away the tacky streaks, steadied herself, and shook out her hands. "I guess I can't use my magic here."

"Yeah. We're lucky the whole flat didn't explode."

She scanned the wreckage. Her gaze snagged on the limp thread of white near her boot; she nudged it gently. It collapsed into fine ash.

"That complicates things," she murmured, exhaling. "Are you hurt?"

"Burns, a few bites. I don't think they were venomous."

She nodded once, retrieved her hat from a patch of unburned grass, and beat the ash from the brim. Then she turned south again, eyes flinty above the mask.

"Then we need to move," she said, voice low. "Without those snakes, Lusin has no way to track us."

CHAPTER 26
BATTLE FOR THE KEY

The sounds of battle carried far through the still air. James sprinted between the granite stones toward the source, Sarah close behind. The ground trembled beneath his boots, each quake punctuated by flashes of light and thunderous impacts that shattered the silence.

He knew Lusin was fighting the key guardian. He pushed himself harder, lungs burning, heart pounding with terror and hope. Lusin needed him—needed him *now*.

He burst from the last of the stones into a clearing at full speed. The sight before him made him skid to a halt so suddenly that Sarah almost crashed into him. He barely noticed. He could only stare, transfixed and horrified, trying to understand what he was seeing.

Two creatures were locked in combat at the center of the blasted field. The boulders scattered around them had been split and flung apart as if by a storm of magic and fury.

One was monstrous—huge and hunched, its body matted with coarse black hair and patches of sickly green skin. Its muscles bulged grotesquely, giving it a bear-like shape in silhouette only. Its squashed face was split by a wide, crooked smile full of yellow teeth and dripping blood. Its bloodshot red eyes gleamed with madness.

But the other creature—James's breath caught. It was smaller, almost human in shape, yet impossibly beautiful and terrifying.

Its lower body was serpentine, a long white tail that coiled and lashed through the dirt. Scales like polished marble gleamed across its hips, shoulders, and arms, fading into smooth, pale skin at the chest and throat. Each finger ended in needle-like long claws stained dark with the guardian's blood.

Its youthful face was framed by glittering scales along its temples and cheeks, and long white hair whipped in an unseen wind. Twin fangs glinted over his lips as his eyes—red as burning coals—flared with fury.

Magic coiled around him in waves of acid green, his aura pulsing brighter with every strike.

He was horrifying.

He was magnificent.

He was *Lusin.*

James stumbled forward on the shaking earth, voice cracking.

"Lusin…?"

Despite the din, the name reached him. The serpent's glowing eyes shifted from red to gold as his head snapped toward the sound. For an instant, his deadly aura faltered. His face went through a cascade of emotions—shock, disbelief, awe, pain, relief.

"James," he breathed, the word sounding like a prayer.

Their fragile reunion was shattered by manic cackling.

The beast was laughing.

"That's it! He sees you now, Lusin!" it howled, its cracked flesh peeling into a wider grin. "He sees the monster you *really* are! And it will be the last thing he ever sees!"

James's gaze locked with the creature's blood-red eyes. His body siezed—utterly. He couldn't blink, couldn't breathe, couldn't move. Panic clawed through him, but his body refused to obey.

The guardian lunged. Its massive claws sliced through the air, the distance closing in a heartbeat.

Then—a blinding flash.

A blur of white intercepted the strike.

The sound of impact was a sickening *crunch*.

Hot blood sprayed across James's face. The spell snapped, and he collapsed to his knees just in time to catch Lusin as he fell.

He barely heard Sarah shouting his name. The world had narrowed to the weight in his arms. Lusin's body was changing, the serpent form fading back into the shape James knew. His shirt and body was shredded from hip to shoulder, and crimson poured from the deepest gash along his ribs. Even though he knew it was useless, he pushed his hand into the wound trying to stem the flow of life leaving Lusin's body.

"Lusin… why?" James whispered, his voice breaking.

"James… I—" Lusin tried to speak, but blood welled at his lips. Trembling, he lifted one blood-slicked hand to James's cheek. His skin was ice-cold.

"No… no, you're going to be okay!" James said quickly, half pleading, half commanding. "We'll get you help, I promise!"

Lusin smiled faintly. His eyes fluttered closed, and his hand slipped from James's face.

"*Lusin?*"

"Lusin!"

James shook him, desperation taking over. His vision blurred with tears, his chest tightening until it hurt to breathe. This couldn't be real. He pressed his face into Lusin's chest and screamed—a raw, guttural sound that ripped through the clearing.

The earth itself seemed to echo his anguish.

Sarah skidded to his side, shouting words he couldn't hear. Her hands gripped his shoulders, shaking him, but her voice was lost in the ringing in his ears.

Then the ground moved.

The air vibrated with a furious growl.

Behind Sarah, the key guardian loomed—larger, darker, more monstrous than before. Its eyes burned like coals, its body swelling with new power.

James barely registered the danger. His grief hollowed him out; all that remained was rage. He rose, swaying, blood and magic burning beneath his skin.

Arcane energy gathered in his right hand—too much, far too much—but he didn't care. He felt it climb up his arm like molten fire, scorching veins and nerves alike.

Sarah screamed his name, clutching at him, but her voice was far away. The power demanded release, and James let it go.

The blast erupted from his palm like a star being born.

Light swallowed the world.

Sound shattered.

Then—silence.

When the world returned, James lay sprawled among the shattered stones. His body burned, but he was alive. Sarah's sobs reached him, and then her hands—grabbing, shaking, dragging him back to awareness.

He groaned and rolled onto his side. Her masked face hovered over him, tear tracks streaking the soot on her cheeks.

"James! Oh thank the gods—you're alive!" she cried, pulling him into a crushing hug.

"Yeah, Sarah… I'll live," he rasped, patting her shoulder weakly until she let go.

He blinked through the haze. The battlefield was a grave-yard of smoke and blue fire. The swamp burned in slow, ghostly rings that hissed against the small pools of dark water. Everything else was ash.

Then he remembered.

"Where's Lusin?!" he shouted, grabbing Sarah's arm.

Her eyes welled again. "I'm sorry, James…" she whispered before breaking into sobs.

James turned, dread coiling through him.

Lusin lay fifteen feet away in a pool of blood.

He scrambled to him, dropping to his knees and gathering the limp body into his arms. Lusin's skin was clammy, his breathing shallow, his heartbeat faint—too faint.

"Lusin? Please, wake up…"

No response.

James's mind raced. There *had* to be something—anything. He dug through his torn pack, his shaking hands finding a small velvet pouch. Sahir's gift. He didn't even remember why he'd kept it.

He tore it open with his teeth.

Inside, the glittering white of powdered basilisk scales caught the light.

Instinct drove him to act while reason agonized. He poured the contents into the wound. For a terrible moment, nothing happened—then the powder began to glow. The particles melted into the blood, flaring green and hissing like acid. Flesh knit together before his eyes.

"Come on, come on…" James muttered as hope began to rise.

The light flared brighter, sealing the gash halfway before fading. He emptied the rest of the pouch, then bound the remaining wound with strips of bandage. Sweat stung his eyes, but hope filled his chest until it was painful.

Sarah knelt beside him, silent, watching as he worked.

"He's going to be okay," James said firmly, half to her, half to himself.

Minutes passed in tense quiet until a weak voice broke through it.

"James?"

James's head snapped up. He stared into golden eyes.

"Lusin!" he gasped, and before he could stop himself, he pulled the serpent prince into a fierce embrace.

Lusin's arms trembled as they circled his waist. James could feel the faint rhythm of his heart, fragile but steady. Relief flooded him so hard it hurt.

He cupped Lusin's face, thumb brushing over smooth scales. Lusin leaned into the touch, his lips curving faintly. The small, familiar rumble—a purring sound—rose in his throat.

Overwhelmed, James pulled off his mask and pressed their lips together.

The contact was desperate, clumsy, perfect. Lusin melted against him, fingers tracing his cheeks and hair. James deepened the kiss, tasting blood, tears, and smoke. His heart pounded so hard it felt like it might break his ribs.

When at last they parted, both gasped for air. Lusin's lips were flushed, his eyes bright with wonder—until they dropped to James's chest. His expression changed to horror.

"James—the curse!" he rasped, struggling to sit up.

James looked down. Black lines crawled up his arm, across his shoulder, spiraling over half his chest and down his leg. The markings pulsed faintly, alive beneath his skin.

"I had no choice," James said quietly. "The guardian almost killed you."

Lusin's gaze softened with both love and fear. "You overtaxed your magic again. It's spreading faster."

He traced the lines with trembling fingers. The marks felt warm, rhythmic—as if they were breathing.

"Did you get the key?" he asked suddenly.

James blinked. He'd completely forgotten. Before he could answer, Sarah stepped forward, holding a shining object.

"Here," she said. "I got it."

Lusin exhaled in relief. "Then there is still hope," he murmured. His hand brushed the sapphire set in the bronze filigree.

Sarah tucked both the Air and Water Keys into her pack. "Can you walk, Lusin? We need to move. This area isn't safe."

"I can," he said softly.

James helped him to his feet, slipping an arm around his waist to steady him. Together, they walked, slow but resolute, toward the edge of the Poisonous Flats.

It was well after nightfall when they finally stopped. James spread a blanket on a patch of dry grass and eased Lusin down. Then, exhausted, he lay beside him. For the first time in three days, he slept.

The night pressed close around them, heavy and damp. The swamp was silent—too silent—as if even the insects dared not breathe. From Sarah's pack, the faint blue glow of the Water Key shimmered beside the Air Key, their pulses beating like twin hearts.

Sarah took the first watch. She sat near the fading fire, her eyes drifting to the two sleeping figures. James's arm was curled protectively around Lusin, the black markings on his skin faintly luminous in the moonlight. When she reached out, the air tingled near them—alive, hungry, *aware.* She drew her hand back quickly, whispering an old prayer she barely remembered.

The moon climbed high, casting silver light through the mist. Lusin stirred, his hand tightening on James's sleeve, and the tension in his face eased. For the first time since Dorchas, peace returned—fragile, trembling, but real.

When dawn came, the mist still clung low to the earth. The markings on James's skin had not faded. If anything, they had deepened, sharper and darker, etched into him by an unseen will.

Far to the west, a pillar of light flickered briefly on the horizon—an omen none of them saw. The domain of Earth was stirring. Its guardian had begun to wake.

Sarah tightened the straps of her pack and looked once more at James and Lusin.

"You saved us," she whispered, "but at what cost?"

The two keys in her bag glowed faintly in answer. Their light pulsed together, steady and soft, before fading into the dawn.

Beneath the waking world, far below the Poisonous Flats, something vast and ancient stirred.

And in the depths of the earth, a single heartbeat answered.

EPILOGUE

Far below the surface of the earth, in a chamber carved of obsidian and bone, Sahir stands before a mirror of living crystal. Inside, faint ripples of light mark the motion of something vast—veins glowing through rock like the breath of a buried god.

A whisper crawls up from the depths.

"Two locks open. The pulse quickens."

Sahir presses his cursed hand to the glass; black veins flare across his skin.

"Not yet awake," he murmurs, "but dreaming louder."

Behind him, runes ignite—records of hosts long dead, vessels that failed. James's name glows newest, brightest.

"The vessel ripens," Sahir says. "When the fourth key turns, the Heart will remember its own."

Far above, on the surface, James jolted awake beside a dying campfire. The rune on his palm glowed red-gold, echoing the rhythm of something beating deep beneath the world.

He does not yet know that what stirs below is listening—and waiting for his body to become its own.

www.ingramcontent.com/pod-product-compliance
Lightning Source LLC
Chambersburg PA
CBHW070855160726
48004CB00003B/1094